"Run Wild, Run Free"

DAVID ROOK

(Original title: The White Colt)

SBS SCHOLASTIC BOOK SERVICES
NEW YORK TORONTO LONDON AUCKLAND SYDNEY

Copyright © 1967 by David Rook. This edition is published by Scholastic Book Services, a division of Scholastic Magazines, Inc., by arrangement with E. P. Dutton & Co., Inc.

3rd printing December 1969   Printed in the U.S.A.

For my parents

from Dr. John Morrisey, M.B., D.P.M., to Miss
Anne Vernon, M.A.

Request for Psychological Testing

Philip Ransome, aged 6 years 5 months.

The initial interview showed that he is clearly
disturbed. At no time did he make any attempt at
speech. He showed signs of distress at unexpected
noises and became anxious if attention was focused upon him.

With regard to the parents it is quite clear that
their relationship is strained. I get the impression
that the mother plays the dominant role and I
would suggest that she may have made too many
emotional demands on the child.

REPORT:

from Miss Anne Vernon, M.A. to Dr. John Morrisey.

PHILIP RANSOME

PSYCHOLOGICAL TESTING

Date of birth: 27.1.49. Parents: James and Ellen Ransome.
Age: 6 years 5 months.
Date of Examination: June 14th, 1955.
When Philip came for Psychological Testing in June 1955 it was hoped to make some assessment of his level of general intelligence and of his capabilities.

Personal History:

Philip's progress during infancy was apparently normal. He spoke his first word at the age of 1 year and could sing nursery rhymes at 2. His speech development up to the age of 5 years was relatively normal apart from a tendency to stammer, which appeared around the age of 3½ years. This condition worsened progressively until around the age of 5 years when he began to withdraw and gradually ceased to make any attempt to communicate with those around him.

By the age of 6 years he was virtually without speech, although he could understand what was said to him. His parents claim that he was "emotionally cold" towards them and that he preferred to play alone rather than with other children.

There is no history of epilepsy, and E.E.G. records show no positive evidence of abnormality.

Philip's behaviour in the test situations was comparative with the description given by his parents. He has spoken only a few words and seems to be frightened by loud and sudden noises.

Psychological Investigations:

Philip is a slender blue-eyed child with brown hair. When he came for testing he was not shy and showed a lively interest in the test materials on the desk.

Unfortunately it has not been possible to obtain any reliable estimate of Philip's I.Q. Luria's work indicates that lack of speech (i.e., language) development tends to retard cognitive function. Philip is undoubtedly suffering from severe retardation, probably induced by emotional strain. Because of his apparently autistic withdrawal and lack of cooperation in various tasks, it was not possible to estimate his intelligence with any accuracy.

One has the impression that Philip is alert and

aware of his surroundings. In his case the under-lying emotional stresses must be remedied before progress can be made on an intellectual level.

Part of a letter from Dr. Morrisey to Mr. and Mrs. Ransome, dated June 25th, 1955:

I believe that it will be of great value to Philip if he be allowed to attend at the clinic so that we can try to help him with some of his difficulties. If you agree, I would suggest that he comes twice weekly for therapy, which will probably continue for some weeks. These problems take time to resolve, as you will realise, but I am sure that we can help your son.

There is one aspect of the situation which I feel I must mention: Children react strongly to the atmosphere in the home. Even in the absence of open quarrels and disagreements, a strained relationship between the parents can cause untold damage. Philip is a very sensitive child and I believe that he is finding it increasingly difficult to cope. I cannot urge you too strongly to see that there is a relaxed atmosphere in the home in which no demands are made upon him. While he is undergoing therapy it is essential that you treat him in a relaxed and accepting way.

July 29th, 1955

Greylands
Hexworthy

Dear Dr. Morrisey,

This is to let you know that I shall not be bringing Philip to the clinic any more.

My husband and I believe that the treatment is having no effect at all and as the journey into Exeter is so difficult for me we have agreed that it is best to call it off.

Thank you very much for trying to help.

Yours sincerely,
Ellen Ransome.

Extract from letter from Miss Anne Vernon, M.A., to Dr. John Morrisey, M.B., D.P.M.

Thank you for the copy of Mrs. Ransome's letter. I wonder whether she will ever fully realise what she is doing to the poor child? Sometimes I despair.

Letter enclosed with Philip Ransome's end-of-term report, dated July 18th, 1964.

Dear Mrs. Ransome,

Now that Philip is fifteen I feel that we cannot

possibly cope with him any longer. I am sure that you are aware that we are under-staffed, and in a large class Philip cannot be given enough of the individual attention he requires.

I must remind you that I have repeatedly advised you to place him in a special school, and I still believe that he would have improved considerably had you done so.

I now suggest that you contact the Education Officer about the boy's future. I have informed the department that I am no longer able to take him here.

Yours sincerely,
H.S. Taylor.

Pure is the white pony
Who lies in the empty valley
With a bundle of fresh hay.
He is like a piece of jade.

Oh, do not be like gold or jade.
Do not go far from my heart!

(from *The Book of Songs*,
probably compiled by Confucius,
translated in *The White Pony*,
edited by Robert Payne, published
by Allen and Unwin, 1947)

Run Wild, Run Free

CHAPTER I

He crouched behind a clump of heather, one arm stretched out before him, his hand clutching a tuft of moor-grass, the knuckles white with strain. A little way off a group of ponies grazed, their backs to the wind that swept across Bairdown towards the heart of the moor.

They were a nondescript bunch. As far back as man can remember stallions have run loose on the moor: Shetland, Welsh, Exmoor, even Arab and cold-blooded breeds, all have flowed into the mainstream. But the Dartmoor stamp has remained strangely pure; not as a standard, a levelling influence, but now and again, every so many foals, a brown pony appears with dense, fine mane and tail, with narrow shoulders and sloping rump, fine-boned but hard, with little flat knees and chiselled hocks, long coated, kind eyed, dainty hooved, and with minute ears, so small as to be disproportionate, lost in the mane that covers the face and neck and hangs almost to the knees.

But the pony that the boy watched was not one of these. This was a foreigner, like a Viking amongst dark-skinned Indians, almost white with an underlay of ochre, mane standing up defiant, and forelock swept aside out of the way of two eyes of palest blue.

It was the eyes that had scorched into the boy weeks before, when he had burst from behind a pile of granite slabs on the side of Bellever to stumble on this pony. They had faced each other, the two of them, while the burning blue eyes of the colt challenged his own. Then the colt exploded in a stiff-legged leap of terror that scattered the group; the boy's eyes followed the white pony until it disappeared in the March murk of the descending ground towards Brimpts and Watersmeet. He had been stunned by the impact of those strange eyes and had started to follow the track of the frightened ponies, but they had disappeared. They moved on and away in fits and starts of fear, as though pursued by the wind.

He returned late that first night, exhausted but excited. His mother had roamed the house anxiously, worried by his absence, but at the sound of the latch she dropped immediately into a chair and feigned absorption in a book. He entered the room silently. His father lowered his newspaper a fraction, looked briefly towards him and then raised the paper again. She did not dare look at the boy. She had learned from many defeats how to control her feelings and remained motionless. Yet tonight was different from all the others. Instead of passing silently on the way to his bedroom to await whatever food and drink she

18

would prepare for him, he came to the far side of the table from where she sat and stood facing her. She raised her eyes from the book and saw his hand, which rested on the green baize covering the table. It was twitching, the fingers curling round imaginary grass-stalks and then making tentative movements towards her, only to draw back and curl again. She watched his hand for a few moments, fascinated. There was a sound from his throat; she looked up to his eyes: They were looking straight down into hers. She felt tired suddenly and helpless.

She said quietly: "What is it, Philip?"

There was a rustle as the man in the armchair by the fire lowered his newspaper again.

"What is it, son?" she repeated gently, not insisting; suffering had made her wise. He leaned forward, then recovered jerkily, looked down at the table-top and up into her hooded eyes again. There was something between them, fighting for breath in the emptiness between their eyes, but the distance was too much. There was too much in the way between them.

He broke suddenly, turned away from her and blundered out of the room and up the stairs. She sat motionless for a moment and then moved silently in his wake to stand outside his closed door, listening helplessly to the dry sobbing that came from his room. She stayed until he had finished and slept, and then went back to the silent room; she sat down at the table, put her head down on to her forearms and wept herself. The man who sat in the armchair by the still-glowing fire froze into total embarrassment.

Only the clock on the mantelpiece ticked cheerfully in the hushed room.

During the days that followed Philip searched for the pony with the impossible eyes, casting wide across all the open moor. Watersmeet and Yar Tor, round to the moorgate at Hexworthy and on to Combestone Tor, the wastes of Fox Tor, back to Bellever and Saddle Tor and Laughter Tor, then the big step across the Two Bridges road and the immensities that are borne against the stream of the West Dart below White Tor, past the tangled silence of Wistman's Wood and on to Bairdown, Crow Tor, Vixen Tor and the central plateau where the rainclouds die.

He came across the horses again some five days later, quiet now, cropping sparse turf above Grimspound. He had wandered amongst the shafts and tunnels of the Vitifer mines until the atmosphere of that strange sloping plain had down-daunted him. He had expected to see in the peat-rusted water a flash of white, shining like a star fallen deep into the terrible black shafts; but they were grazing above Grimspound. Remembering their panic-stricken flight at the first encounter he stalked carefully, knowing intuitively that if they sensed his nearness it would be by sight and not by scent. He worked steadily towards them using every scrap of available cover, worming on his progress with a crouching run. Finally he lay, twisted excitedly, to peer out at the white pony.

He did not know why he sought the creature so eagerly; it was enough to see his quarry and he was amazed when a chance movement gave him a glimpse of the blue eyes. He did not know but it was the will to possess that ran like wine in his troubled blood. Through all the years of his childhood his delight had been to see, to hear, to smell and touch, but in the completeness of his inner world he had never once desired to own anything. Now the weight of his growing manhood leaned heavily against him, so that the stirring wild blue eyes of the colt became a love-object, and the colt itself a thing to be possessed.

Suddenly the pony sensed his presence. The clear eyes lifted and stared. Philip rose slowly to his feet and faced the pony square, hands still at his sides, head lifted. The other ponies nearby shied away and trotted a few paces, then turned and gazed, but the white colt stood like a statue, only the blown motion of its thick mane moving. While the boy and the colt stood like this, facing one another, motionless, the other ponies, one by one, dropped their heads again to their grazing and began a slow movement away from the area, quite different from their day's-long flight from him earlier on the slopes of Bellever.

Something was happening between Philip and the white colt, standing there yards apart, specks on the side of the massive hill above the ancient stone village. The chosen rook knows before the falcon stoops.

There are understandings between men and animals, too many and too strong to be denied.

So the first phase of one of these strange associations began. The boy had been instantly fascinated by this fey creature and had pursued and found it; and now as hunter and quarry faced each other, a current flowed from one to the other as palpably as sound waves shaking a flame. Along this current the boy's fascination seemed to flow, into the blue eyes and the very nerves of the colt. Suddenly the boy felt drained, empty, watchful, while the colt could not get away. It moved a couple of times as if seeking a way to escape: shook its head, pawed the ground nervously, even snatched at a tuft of grass, but the jaws worked without rhythm. Once or twice it threw up its head and gazed after its companions, now indistinct towards the bottom of the valley, and neighed after them with a shrill note of pleading, but still the colt could not leave.

The midday wore away. The boy sat back against a projecting rock, forearms resting on raised knees, not knowing what he was doing, just waiting. The colt waited too, relaxed now, its companions gone and forgotten. Its blue eyes regarded the boy with a sidelong curiosity, and although it cropped the grass, it moved in a slow circle about Philip as if attached to him by a line.

The colt's grazing brought it gradually nearer to Philip, who sat still, turning his head only to follow its course until losing sight as the colt passed beyond the rock at his back; and here the colt became strangely restive and hurried on its way until it entered again the sphere of the boy's eyes, then relaxed and resumed its slow, warm regard of the waiting figure. By the time the light had begun to fade a little, the colt was tearing at the tough fibrous grass-stalks almost at Philip's feet. As it tore and chewed, tore and chewed, it seemed to settle into a stance. This change in the animal's movements elicited an immediate response in Philip who remained still, but drew his mind in from the extremities of his body, the pores of his skin. He felt a sense of transition from passivity to a positive action, but it was the colt who brought about the first gentle crisis. By degrees it ceased grazing and, for the first time since its initial frightened stare, looked him full in the face from both its enchanted eyes. Slowly and with little nervous starts it stretched forward its head until Philip felt warm breath on the skin of his ankle, above the sock. Suddenly he wanted to leap and shout, to see the beast rear in terror with staring eyes and flying mane — it was a momentary reaction of fear, but he quelled it in a second and forced himself to relax progressively through every fibre of his body. He nearly shouted as the colt brushed its nostrils against his foot and started back in sudden fear, but the eyes lost their wildness immediately and it rocked forward off its hocks and continued its nasal exploration of the hunched figure before it. Minutes before the flared nostrils arrived at his face he knew what he had to do. He breathed in for the first time the blood-warm breath, then raised his head and gently blew his answer direct into the pony's consciousness. The colt stood still for a moment, and Philip breathed once more, carefully, into the quivering nostrils. The colt inhaled once, sharply, and raised its head with a

23

rippling sound from its throat. It pulled familiarly at a lock of Philip's hair that had lain across his forehead all afternoon. From deep within the boy a spring of exultation gushed upwards, forcing all the breath from his lungs as it passed, rushing up his throat like liquid fire and slamming against the inside of his forehead, pushing at the back of his eyeballs until they ached. If he could have shouted, the intolerable pressure would have eased, but he could not, so he put his head back until it strained against the rock behind him and waited for the waves to end their battering inside his skull, his eyes unseeing, turned inwards and drowning.

It passed quickly. The boy felt weak, his limbs trembling as they relaxed. A movement against his arm recalled him: The pony was exploring him with its warm breath. As he watched, it took a tentative step forward and he moved his leg in time to avoid being trodden. It loomed over him now, brushing his shoulders, his neck, with its muzzle; he could feel the coarse hairs on its upper lip against his ear and stifled a desire to laugh. He stretched out his hand and touched the leg that rose from the ground beside him: The pony did not flinch. He ran his hand down from the knee, over the cool straight cannon bone, the tips of his fingers following the twin tendons along their tensile length, into the swelling of the fetlock; he paused to twist his fingers gently in the long hairs that enveloped the ergot, then slid his hand down to the slope of the pastern; he closed his grip until the tip of his second finger just touched his thumb and held his breath in sudden

24

wonder when tendons leapt into play on either side as the pony altered its stance; he stroked the coronet where the silver-white coat ended in a fine fringe over the curved wall of the hoof, descending hard and flawless from its matrix. He sat still then, his hand resting on the cool hoof, while the pony continued its process of familiarisation with the smells of his body and his clothes. As he sat, half-formed thoughts jostled in his mind, fragments of disjointed speech, struggling momentarily for expression before sinking into oblivion: "pony . . . dark line down the . . . long hairs, one in my eye, tickles . . . pony, pony . . . green belly, shadow . . . hot down my neck, pony . . ." and the pony was breathing him in, his essence, his half-sweet, half-sour life of milk and meat. The boy rose to his feet. The colt stood, bland in the level sunlight.

"Philip," the boy said.

CHAPTER II

THEY LIVED AT HEXWORTHY, a village near the
edge of Dartmoor. James Ransome was a solicitor
in Ashburton, ten miles away; he drove himself
to work each day, going in by way of Dartmeet
and New Bridge, returning through Holne and
over Combestone Tor.

To James Ransome the moor was a tireless
enemy as it rolled down and lipped with patient
aggression at the careful cultivation of his vege-
table garden.

But the boy it had taken to its heart. As soon
as he could crawl he would orient towards the
magnetic centre of the moor: Time and time
again he was retrieved crawling steadily and
grimly up the long slope away from the house.
After a while they had erected a fence to stop
him. This he would attack with an absorbed concentration so that the fence, assailed from one
side by his cunning fingers and from the other by
the sympathising moor, would collapse in upon

itself, falling neither one way nor the other, but somehow inwards; it was as though the forces holding it up had disintegrated rather than the materials of which it was made. So they locked him in his room. He would climb on to a chair and attain the windowsill, clinging with tireless fingers to see out across the wastes, watching the fleeting cloud-shadows, the curlews and the soaring buzzards. He would drink the landscape in like sustenance. When his mother came in he would turn upon her his eyes full of distance and she would flinch away from them, busying herself with tasks and talking to frighten away the emptiness.

Throughout the penance of his schooldays the moor had been his solace and his sanctuary. Awkward and silent amongst his fellow-beings, the boy became transformed as he ran through the sparkling heather and lay breathless in the cotton grass. At such time he would seem to sing to the moor, making sounds to it formed half of words and half of colours and smells. And not only his voice but also his limbs became suddenly and rapturously free; too long, too impetuous, too careless for classroom and drawing-room, they became in one leaping transition the legs of a colt kicking caprioles in the air, running with dazzling swiftness down long grey hillsides, his arms held out, away from his sides, like young wings testing the wind.

On his release from school at the age of fifteen he had found himself completely free at last. He would wander all day across the moors, returning to eat when hunger compelled him, and at night to sleep.

An engima to his parents before, he became a total stranger now. His mother, driven to exasperation by his intangibility, would lock him in sometimes and stand outside the door of his room. She would wait for him to show some sign of reaction, of rebellion or sorrow, so that she could unlock the door and go to him on human terms; but at times such as these he would be silent and acquiescent, sitting silently on the floor, his wrists round his bony knees, his eyes fixed on a point a little in front of his feet. Only when she stood over him and shouted at him in her loneliness and incomprehension would there be a reaction: His face would twist into its familiar grimace and his arms would wrap themselves closer around him.

After each spell of imprisonment he accepted his rewon freedom with an indiscriminate gratitude, almost as though he lacked insight into cause and effect and failed to associate his curtailed freedom with his mother's will. As he walked gently past her and out into the air he seemed to radiate this undirected gratitude; she would drink it in, thirsting as she was for love.

So he had come to his sixteenth year, beginning to grow a little, yet slender and somehow fragile. People would speak kindly to him, passing him in the village, and he would walk carefully by, his head averted. Some thought of him as a sort of idiot, but they were wrong. In spite of his inability to communicate with his own kind, he had absorbed far more than anyone at that time ever realised. By means of a purely one-way process he had almost managed to grow up; he had accumulated both academic knowledge and practical skills; most incredible of all, his character, his own shape as a person, had somehow managed to develop, without ever being seen by anyone. Even his turning to the moors was a flight from something desired to something familiar, as though his need to communicate had been too great to bear, rather than not strong enough.

And now, in his sixteenth year, the slow process of maturation within him had paused as though to gather strength. He could feel the pressure as his own future was held, straining towards release. He was like a falcon come to maturity in captivity, tethered to the ground, with flight coursing through its wings; only a knot kept him from the sky.

It would be hard to say exactly when Philip first met the moorman. "Met," anyway, is the wrong word: the tall spare figure of the old man was as much a part of the moors as the rocks themselves. A relationship had grown between him and the boy simply because they were so often in the same place at the same time, and shared the same sense of wonder. He was also Lt-Col. Jonathan Lane-Forster, M.C., Ph.D., but people called him "the moorman."

In his prime he had been a tall straight tree; sixty-one years had shrunk him a little and weathered him much, but they had left his skin a ruddy brown which emphasised the grizzled white of his close-cropped hair and moustache, and even more his clear grey eyes. His face was scored and hewn by deep lines, very much like the weathering on the tors he loved; yet, for all that, it was a face that combined strength and age with kindness and a quality of childish wonder.

This April morning spring was exploding in hedgerows and spinneys with yellows, whites, and sap-greens; insects were beginning to hone the air; early butterflies blundered, still drunk with sleep.

On the moor spring was working too, but subtly, with none of the infectious bustle and buzz of the high-banked lanes of the in-country. Here on the rolling slopes of heather and whortleberry it was a force that heaved imperceptibly in the black peat, that twisted amongst the woody stems of heather and clumps of moor-grass. There were fewer flowers here, and so fewer insects: only heavy fuel-tanked dor beetles, lean aerobatic dragon-flies, a few slow biplane bees on reconnaissance flights. On the shadowed earth beneath the heather ran emerald-green tigers with pink spots like warning-signals; in their dark coiling knots, sleeping vipers stirred, blackness flickering within their lidless eyes.

The moorman walked across the broad face of Bellever. His progress was slow, for the ground was broken and rocks abundant. He paused for a moment to breathe in the cool dry breeze and looked up to his left where the slope of the tor rose gently to the round granite pile at the top, like the breast of a sleeping girl. Majestic cloud banks rose beyond the summit while smaller, whiter clouds hurried overhead, casting fleeting shadows across the grey and green wastes.

He sighed with pleasure at the newness and the age of everything, then walked on again, helping himself with an ash stick. While the vast sky and the rolling distances of the moor soaked into him, his eyes were directed downward, seeking a sudden movement or a speck of colour out of context.

After his retirement and the death of his wife he had hidden himself away, barricaded in his lonely cottage, fighting off the silent hordes of memory. But he was too wise and too well-balanced a human being to remain long beseiged; and so, after a time, he opened his doors and his windows to people and the sweet air, and opened his heart in welcome to memory and to solitude. Between leaving the Regular Army and the outbreak of the Second World War he had taught botany and zoology at a public school, and now at last everything clicked into place and he began to wander out on to the moors. At first he could see no farther than the original objects of his interest: the local flora and fauna; but as he ranged farther from his home, he became increasingly aware of the altering character of the moors. At first he noticed only the scientific clues: how one patch of moor dominated by heather would suddenly give way to another where clumps of whortleberry littered the moor-grass; how the bracken was making inroads into

31

old stands of heather; how snails were scarce where the soil lacked calcium, and so on. But as the seasons drifted like cloud-shadows across his life, he began to sense the character of the moor as being something deeper altogether than these manifestations; at last he felt his blood begin to course in rhythm with some ancient heart beating deep within the black peat at the centre of the moor. He began to read the moors, to learn their moods, their changing conditions; he began to live with the moors as a man lives with a woman: a process of give and take, of breaking down and building up; he began, at last, truly to live, which is to love. Strange how happiness can arrive late and unheralded and settle into a man's waking and sleeping and breathing. He who had grown old and stern through loss and disillusion became suddenly gentle and hopeful, and it was because of this that he was the only human being to whom the boy could talk.

A great, flat boulder projected on a rising angle from the mass of clitter that clothed the slopes of Bellever. The moorman stood his stick against it and knelt to study a maidenhair spleenwort growing from a fissure in the rock's side: long, fine stalks with brilliant green leaves pressed close to each other on either side. A movement caught his eye, he lost it, then found it again: a grasshopper. The patched browns and olives showed him that it was a myrmeleotettix, which was sufficiently unusual on that part of the moor for him to note it down on a pad he kept for the purpose. He searched carefully through the whortleberry at the base of the rock but uncovered nothing more. He was reaching for his stick to move on when something else caught his attention, on the horizon this time. Where the gentle swell of Bellever made a slow curve against the sky before sinking into the upsurge of Laughter Tor, something was moving: a mote of white, gleaming sparklike in the fitful sunlight. He took his field glasses from their case and focused them until the dancing blur resolved itself into a white pony. He was about to lower the glasses when his eye caught a movement at the periphery; he shifted the glasses through half a degree or so and Philip Ransome leapt clear and hard to the centre of his vision, his hair blowing wild, his lips moving and an expression of anguish on his face that was obvious even at that range. The moorman stood motionless for a few seconds, then slowly lowered the glasses and put them away. After standing for a little while, his head bent in thought, he took up his stick and began to walk steadily towards the brow of Bellever where the distraught boy shouted words to a white pony which were swallowed by the distance.

A week before, Philip and the white pony had had their second meeting and their friendship had begun. The pony had followed him home, walking close and often breaking into a little trot in order

33

to keep up, for the boy moved with long, loose strides. When at last they had seen the lights of the village appearing one by one over the final slope it was so dark that he could only see a pale blur close behind him. That night Philip lay awake, waiting for the dawn to show him whether or not the pony had gone. Two or three times he got out of bed and crossed to the open window to peer out into the sighing darkness, but there was no moon. As the first dimness crept into the sky he fell into a brief deep sleep, to wake with a start an hour later, his heart beating wildly; his staring eyes took in the blue sky and the light-flooded room for one disbelieving moment, then he leapt from his bed, whimpering, and ran to the window: The pony was grazing calmly a hundred yards away.

Those first few days he lived in a sun-drenched world of wonder. It was one of those early romances between the sun and the moor when everything is gentle and warm, before the sun learns how to kill as well as revivify. Philip and the pony wandered aimlessly, the pony grazing much of the time, Philip lying on the ground, his head resting on his back-flung arms, gazing at it. From time to time the pony would cease to graze and would look at Philip from beneath long white lashes, and Philip would feel his heart contract, as if in pain.

He had not thought about what he wanted of the pony, it simply did not occur to him. He lived each moment in a sort of ecstasy of sensation and slept warm in the certainty of the white pony glimmering outside his window. He woke one morning before dawn, dressed eagerly and crept swiftly down the stairs, shoes in hand, to the back door and out into the breathless stillness from which the dew was still settling. The pony was standing asleep, one hind leg resting, so that dew drops reflected the moonlight from the slope of its quarters. It gave no sign as Philip approached and continued its even breathing as the boy pressed himself against it, hands tangling in its mane. They were both under the spell of the stillness peculiar to the pre-dawn at this time of year: spellbound by the coldness of the air and their own warmth, by the immense breathing silence that seemed to envelop them, cutting them off from the rest of the world. The boy pushed his fingers into the pony's coat, stooped to lay his cheek against its neck, then turned so that his face was buried in the fine mane, his free hand stroking along the smooth neck, then following the bone down to the point of the shoulder as if learning it by heart. All the while the pony's eyes were pools of shadow, the lids half-closed, the lashes heavy with dew.

Each day the pony led the boy a little farther afield, but followed him willingly each evening when he returned home. On the seventh day, however, there was a change in the pony's behaviour. When Philip went out just after seven he could not see it. He stopped for a moment, disbelieving, then ran to the gate in the fence and looked out on to the moor. The pony was there: not asleep or peacefully grazing as usual but trotting up the slope on the moor, head high and mane flying. A sound floated back to him:

the colt was calling to something or someone and there was a wild ring to its voice. As he watched, it stood for a moment like a statue looking away over the moor, then turned with a toss of its head and trotted back towards him, its tail streaming out like that of a comet. Philip went through the gate, closing it behind him, and out on to the moor. When the pony saw him it broke into a gallop. The boy drew in his breath sharply and stood dumbfounded as the colt galloped towards him, veering and leaping over rocks and tussocks, its mane and tail flying. As it drew near it slowed to a raking trot; Philip could see its sides heaving and hear the snorting of its breath, the nostrils showing blood-red at their centre. The colt scattered to a halt before him, almost barging into him; its eyes were wild and staring. It blew violently into his hand and stood trembling with little nervous movements of its head. Philip tried to soothe it, and indeed the pony did quieten, the trembling stopped; but then he would feel the muscles tense beneath his hand and the white head would swing up and fix, the pale blue eyes engulfing the horizon in their demented stare.

Nothing terrible happened. The boy watched the colt ceaselessly but it settled to graze sporadically between short bouts of walking. Yet soon he noticed that they were already as far from home as they had been on any previous day, and still the colt grazed and walked, grazed and walked, like a clockwork toy. Philip tried to halt or even slow the pony's progress, but he could not; he tried sitting down and refusing to move, but the colt drifted steadily away from him until it was almost out of sight, and he panicked and ran after it, distraught.

They had moved along the bank of the Dart as far as Swincombe Meet, where the pony forded the stream, the boy following by way of the stepping stones; up the hill looking across to Sherberton, across the road and on to the slopes of Bellever. The boy was desperate now, feeling his happiness going, unable to communicate again. He tried standing in front of the pony and preventing it forcibly from moving on, but it looked at him mildly and walked on, pushing him gently but definitely to one side. He stood looking after it, stooping slightly, his arms stiff at his sides, fists clenched. Tears welled up behind his eyes and something tore within him: he closed his eyes and shouted: "Philip!" The breeze tore at the sound and it reached the colt in little fragments; it froze for a second, then moved on, still grazing, its jaws working rhythmically. The boy shouted again, the tears running down his face now: "Phillip!" And suddenly the colt did stop — swung its head suddenly and stood at gaze, ears pricked forward. The boy felt hope leap, then realised that it had seen something. He looked in the same direction and saw nothing for a moment, then the head of a man followed by the shoulders as he approached over the swell of the hillside. He stared, trying to identify, then looked back for the pony but it was moving again, this time walking steadily and with such purpose away from him that he could stand no more; a shutter fell in his mind and he slumped to the ground in a kind of stupor of incredulity

37

no longer looking after the receding pony but pulling at grass-stalks.

So he was when the moorman walked slowly up to him. Philip looked up vaguely on his arrival, then his eyes fell again as his fingers pulled and tore and his lips worked silently.

Few people realised that Philip was able to speak to the moorman with only a little stammering in his speech. The one chose not to talk about it, the other could not. Philip's mother knew, and the moorman passing their house would feel her eyes resting heavy upon him; but not with malice, he knew, only a sort of wondering sorrow that his diffidence could call forth what her love could not. But now the moorman spoke to Philip and got no reply, no reaction even. He spoke again: "Philip." This time the boy looked up and the moorman held his gaze as he knelt down before him.

"What's the matter, lad?" His voice gentle, as if he were talking to a half-wild animal. "Can't you tell me?"

The boy's eyes cleared, became deep and tortured, his face twisted as if in an epileptic fit and words fought screaming in that poor skull to be released; but only sounds and drops of saliva escaped. Again tears overflowed the impassioned eyes. The old man was moved, but he remained motionless while the boy fought his battle, blinded now by his tears; fought, and finally lost. He closed his eyes and gave a single gasping inarticulate cry of agony, then fell forward and cried as though there were no stopping, ever. The moorman sat down beside the prone

38

figure, rested a hand lightly on the boy's shoulder and waited.

The crying was good. So battered by his emotions had he been that his mind had simply withdrawn, leaving him for the moment an idiot, plucking at grass-stems with white dead fingers. But the old man's childlike grey eyes had pierced the mist in the boy's brain and now the horror and the anguish were pouring out of him like a river in spate, instead of building up inside him into a pressure that might have become intolerable. Gradually the thin shoulder beneath the moorman's hand became still, and at last the boy lay quiet, one cheek pressing against the dark peat, his eyes open, dirt on his face. The moorman sensed that for the boy to be able to talk to him now there must be no physical contact between them, so he removed his hand and looked away towards the horizon. When he spoke again it was with a careful indifference.

"Do you feel better now?"

There was no reply. It came to him in a flash of insight. "It's the pony, isn't it, lad?"

The boy said nothing, but the old man saw an affirmative movement of the head.

"Tell me about it."

The boy sat up and looked once in the direction in which the pony had gone, searching the horizon, then looked down again, composed now.

"He's m-m-mine."

"A present from your parents?"

"No."

"Who gave him to you?"

A pause, then, "N-no-one."

39

The moorman began to understand.

"Did you find him, Philip?"

The boy nodded, almost eagerly.

"I see; when was this?"

The boy had to think a moment: when?

"Last week."

"Where were you keeping him?"

The boy made a vague gesture with one hand to say: here, of course. On the moor.

"I see."

He pieced it all together in his mind: the pony staying in the vicinity of the house, the boy happy with his new companion, happy with something to care for; then the wanderlust returning, the pony drifting restlessly farther and farther from the house, the boy following distraught, and finally hopeless. In the same moment he realised that the boy had nowhere to keep the pony; that anyway he had no right to it — there would be a brand, of course; that the parents might object; all this he reviewed, briefly and objectively. But he was going to help the boy to find and to keep his lost pony. Somehow. He sighed once, before saying quietly, "I'll help you find him, lad."

The boy nodded quickly without looking up, as though he had already known that the moorman would help him. Perhaps he did know, thought the old man in sudden surprise, and smiled at the thought. From the corner of his eye he saw the boy steal a shy glance at him and then look down again.

"We'll work out a plan of campaign; organise it properly. Don't worry, lad," he said, looking at the boy again, "we'll find him." The boy looked up, his eyes shining, and nodded, wordlessly.

"By the way, what do you call him?"

"Philip," the boy said quickly.

The moorman was startled. He was silent for a while, trying to solve this new puzzle.

"But why 'Phillip' especially?" he asked. "That's your name."

The boy considered for a moment.

"I d-d-don't know," he replied, then, "perhaps b-b-because he's l-l-like me."

The old man still wondered.

"How is he like you?"

The boy thought again, then looked up, squinting up at the old man, a smile on his lips that was almost mischievous.

"B-because he's d-different from the others," he said.

The old man stared at him for fully five seconds, startled out of his composure, then looked away with a chuckle. My God, he thought, I shall never get used to this boy. One minute he's a tearful kid and the next minute he comes out with a remark like that . . . He sat for a few moments more, then sighed and got up stiffly, reaching down for his stick.

"Come along, lad," he said.

CHAPTER III

T HEY SEARCHED FOR THE PONY, the moorman
and the boy, but it had disappeared. When they
had covered all the moor within a day's walking
the old man cranked his old car and pressed it
into unwilling service. They went rattling and
squeaking to such places as Widecombe in the
Moor, Moretonhampstead, Chagford, Okehamp-
ton, Yelverton; they went down through the fertile fields around Buckfastleigh and Ashburton;
they combed Holne Moor and the Chase, with
the rushing of waters sounding in their ears beneath the great pines.

The boy stayed, set-faced, in the car while
the moorman made enquiries: old friends who
welcomed him, listened attentively, looked curi-
ously across at the white face behind the closed
windows of the car and went off to start new
searches for the blue-eyed colt.

They found allies at Sherberton, a nearby
farm: John Brookshaw farmed there and he and

his younger sister Diana bred ponies as their family had for well over a century. John was kept busy with the multiple demands of the livestock — as well as the ponies he kept a milking herd of South Devons, a beef herd of Galloways, some hundreds of Black-faced sheep and a few dozen chickens — but he promised to keep an eye open for the white colt during his rides around the newtake. Diana, however, threw herself into it as though she were personally involved, riding out whenever she could to search in the most inaccessible parts of the moor. Although not yet twenty the responsibility of helping John on the farm had given her a calm maturity, yet she was fresh and natural with an easy smile. Like many others she had tried to speak to Philip, without success; but where others had simply put him out of their minds after their failure, Diana still tried, as gently as she knew how, but persistently. Although he could not answer her, nor even look at her properly, Philip had become aware of her warmth and her interest; in her company he was silent but far more relaxed than with other people, the moorman excepted.

There was another ally at Sherberton: old Reg. He was a fierce, ragged little old man who had worked there all his life; a great hooked nose and bushy eyebrows almost hid the eyes which were blue and gentle, like the eyes of a child. He spoke rapidly and with much swearing in the old dialect; when excited, which was often, his speech became quite unintelligible. He loved his employers, John and Diana, with a blind loyalty; over the years he had built up a deep affection

43

for the moorman, and it was because of both of these factors that he, too, joined the search.

"Why, Cunnel," he said to the moorman one day, "thur ben't naw place thiccy pawny could 'ide roand yur. Us'll find un, doan'ee worry, midear."

Weeks passed. The boy became daily more silent, more absent. He would sit upright in the old car as it bounced and yawed, gazing sightlessly ahead, only his eyes flickering as another straggling group of ponies showed itself like flotsam on a grey-green ocean. His mother looked at his face each evening as he came in and read the answer there, then moved silently to fetch his food hot from the oven. It was even harder for her than before because the arrival of the pony had brought the two of them closer together, mother and son. Still he could not speak to her, but he had a positive warmth about him in his waking hours, and she had basked in it. But now the light had gone out of his eyes and hope shrivelled within her.

The search lost momentum. The old man had given up hope and continued only because he dared not destroy the boy; yet the boy seemed not to hope any longer, and showed no emotion when, one evening, the old man said:

"Philip, I can't go out with you for a couple of days — I've been neglecting my affairs and I must catch up on them. Now you rest for a day or two and then we'll carry on the search, all right?"

44

But the hope with which he tried to infuse his words rang false, and he winced at his own strange voice. The boy nodded briefly, got out of the car and walked quickly up the path and in through the door, leaving it half-open. The old man sat, chewing his lip, his hands gnarled like roots on the steering-wheel, deep in thought.

He looked up with a start: The boy's mother was standing at the garden gate, her hands plucking at her skirt. He smiled at her sadly and shook his head once. She looked down at the ground, then up again.

"You're not going to find him, are you?"

He opened the door and got out of the car, bending and stretching his legs to ease the stiffness.

"No," he said, "I think not, Mrs. Ransome."

Again her eyes pleaded with him: "Isn't there anything we can do — my husband and I, I mean?"

"Just be gentle with him. That's all anyone can do for him at the moment."

She nodded, then seemed to sag visibly.

"Oh, Colonel, it's so difficult! I know he's not like the other boys, but we had a sort of friendship. . . ." She hesitated, then went on, "Even though he can't talk — to us — I mean — I could still feel close to him; and sometimes, every now and then, he'd look at me and there was love in his eyes. I knew there was! and when he found that pony, it was getting better and better, I could feel him growing closer to me, but now he's like a stranger — he's dead — he won't even look at me!"

She was crying now, silently, but with terrible force, her strong frame trembling, her knuckles white as she gripped the top of the gate. He waited, helpless, until she had recovered herself, then said:

"You know that I'll do anything within my power to help you. At the moment I can't think of anything except to go on looking for that damned pony. . . ." He had begun to think of the colt with a rising sense of anger, as if it were all the creature's fault; he knew the injustice, even the childishness of this, but it crept into his thoughts and — as now — into his speech, the very unreasonableness of it making him angrier yet. He controlled the sharp current of vindictiveness at once, and went on: "And if we don't find it in the end, he'll just have to get used to it, I'm afraid."

"Is there nothing else we can do?" she asked.

"Not that I know of."

"Isn't there some way of taking his mind off the pony?"

He thought for a moment. "I don't know . . ." he mused, "but it's worth thinking about." He put his hand on the handle of the car door and stood motionless for a moment, head bent in thought.

"I'll think about it, Mrs. Ransome, I promise," he said, then climbed into the driving seat and slammed the door. He wound the window halfway down: "In the meanwhile, try not to worry too much. The more yourself you can be with him, the easier you'll make it for him. If I think of anything I'll get in touch."

"Thank you, Colonel," she said, "Thank you so much."

The big woman stood there for a while, her face grubby from tears and dust, her eyes following the old car down the road and out of sight. She looked upwards: A tiny speck in the blue emptiness of the evening sky caught her attention — a buzzard soaring high and free on still wings. As she watched, she heard from a great distance its mewing cry, the voice of solitude and despair.

For a few minutes, as something within her reached out and up, her face was that of a girl, her eyes innocent and yearning; for all the pleasant solidity of her body, she felt light and insubstantial, young and ecstatic again. Then her eyes dulled; she sniffed once, rubbed her face with her hands, then turned and walked heavily down the path back to the waiting house.

CHAPTER IV

SOMEONE ELSE SAW THE BUZZARD.

The moorman clambered finally out of his car and leaned back against it as it ticked and hissed in the sudden silence, his eyes following the soaring speck just as the woman's eyes had followed it minutes before. The hawk was a sort of omen, he reflected later, because almost immediately after seeing it he remembered Lady and a plan began to present itself.

Three days later the moorman left home before dawn and drove sedately north. Just after three o'clock that afternoon he pulled up outside a semidetached house in a road on the edge of Blackpool. Before he was through the gate the front door opened and a young man greeted him eagerly:

"Colonel! How are you, sir?"

"Stiff, young man," he replied with a rueful grin, "but very glad to be here."

They shook hands warmly.

"Come on in and have a cup of tea," the young man said, taking the moorman's arm and leading him into the house.

A little later they sat comfortably in the lounge over a second cup of tea. The moorman stretched his legs carefully and sighed. "That's better," he said cheerfully, "my old girl was complaining bitterly at being forced to exceed thirty miles an hour on the M6; I'm sure she'll never take me all the way back again."

"I shouldn't worry, it's nearly all downhill going back," the young man said, "and anyway, you'll stay the night, won't you? You couldn't possibly go back tonight."

"Thank you, Barry, that's very kind, but I'll find myself a hotel somewhere —"

"That's settled then; you'll stay the night."

The moorman hesitated a moment and then surrendered gracefully.

Barry Holliday was twenty-four years old, of medium height and slight build, with a shock of red-brown hair. His voice had a trace of Lancashire, yet it was entirely individual, slow and gentle. What was ordinary about him, living as he did on the outskirts of Blackpool, was that he ran an old car and worked at a nearby factory. What was extraordinary, however, was that he worked night shifts so as to leave the daytime free for his one absorbing passion: Barry Holliday was an accomplished falconer.

"As a matter of fact, if you want to be technical about it, I'm really an austringer," he said with his slow smile, "I'm flying a Gos now."

"Are you now?" said the moorman with some

49

interest, "and how do you find her — is it a female or a tiercel?"

"A female," said Barry. "She's not easy, I must admit, especially after my last peregrine; but she's interesting."

They sat silently for a few minutes, each busy with his own thoughts, then Barry spoke:

"Colonel . . ."

"Yes, lad?"

"Why did you ask me on the phone whether I still had Lady?"

The moorman looked troubled for a moment, then he put down his cup and stood up.

"Let's go for a walk, I could do with a stretch."

"Are you trying to change the subject?" Barry asked, "or are we going for a walk so that you can get your problem off your chest?"

"Yes. Right then, let's be off. Are you going to bring your Gos?"

"No, I've already flown her today. I'll bring Lady, she never bothers about when she goes out or what she does."

They walked down the suburban road and over a stile on to a disused aerodrome; the old man still slightly bent after his long drive, breathing in great draughts of the sea air; the young man walking beside him, his shock of hair blowing across his face, his left forearm held horizontally across his body, the soft leather gauntlet, the sleek kestrel sitting erect on his fist looking eagerly around out of eyes like ebony buttons. Lady.

The moorman told Barry the story of Philip and the blue-eyed colt; told him how the boy was again retiring into his own private world after the loss of the colt; explained how it was that having something to love had been helping the boy to find himself, find his way towards his own kind; explained how the boy's grief was forcing him away again, away from his parents, away from him, the moorman. Then he asked Barry to give Lady to the boy to take the place of the pony.

The young man did not answer straight away. They walked on steadily through the long grass while white clouds chased across the sky, both of them waiting for something. Then Barry stopped, turned into the wind and flicked his left wrist so that the little hawk found herself suddenly airborne; she spread her pointed wings wide and rose sharply against the fresh breeze, then slipped sideways and flapped lazily downwind to alight on an old wooden post about fifty yards away.

Barry reached into his falconer's bag and took out the lure, a stuffed leather pad with a pair of starling's wings attached to it on the end of a long cord. He fiddled with it, his head bent, not looking at the moorman. At last he spoke:

"You know what you're asking, don't you, Colonel?"

"I do," the moorman said, "believe me, I do; and if I didn't believe it to be so important, I should never have dreamed of asking it."

Barry nodded, still fiddling with the lure; then he lifted his head and gazed at Lady perching delicately on the distant stump — the old man looking into his eyes could see the sky and the waving grass reflected there — then he turned, looked straight at the moorman and said, "I think it's a very good idea, Colonel."

The old man could not hold the look and turned away embarrassed, mumbling: "Yes. Yes, I thought you would. That's fine, fine." How could I ask him? he thought: How could I possibly have asked him? But it's done.

"Watch her, Colonel," Barry said sharply as he walked away to a distance of thirty feet or so. He let the lure out a few feet and started to swing it around his head, paying out more line as he did so until the lure was fluttering in a wide circle around him, perhaps two feet above the ground. The moorman, watching the distant shape of the kestrel, saw her freeze and gaze fixedly in their direction; then suddenly she was flying low, straight and fast towards the lure. With incredible speed she covered the distance, and as her course converged rapidly upon the circular track of the lure she veered, gaining ten feet in height, then stooped at it, striking out with her talons. Barry gave the lure an extra boost and the little hawk missed by inches. She threw up immediately, circled twice above their heads on winnowing wings then stooped again: again she missed and this time banked sharply and cut across the circle, flicking Barry's face with one wing as she sliced through the air. The moorman heard a distinct "thwack" and Lady was sitting on her tail, both feet grasping the lure, her perfect wings mantling her catch as though protecting it from the sun. He glanced at Barry and met his eyes. He nodded and looked again at the kestrel, now worrying at a piece of meat attached to the lure. He could say nothing. He could say nothing because he was too full of what he had

52

just been shown: the sheer perfection of the flight of this miniature falcon, this gleaming brown, russet, and cream-coloured hunter. Barry had just shown him what he was being asked to relinquish. But having done this he seemed to accept the idea, and they walked back towards home as though nothing had been asked, talking cheerfully; Lady crouched, wobbling precariously on Barry's fist, ferociously attacking a piece of pigeon wing, a reward for her zeal.

That evening Barry made a box cadge for Lady: a wooden box with padding along the top edge of one side so that she could perch comfortably on the rim. The bootlace that Barry used as a leash would pass through a hole drilled beneath her, and finally a couple of bricks inside the box would hold it down and prevent it from tipping.

After dinner Barry's parents watched television while he and the moorman talked quietly at the other side of the room.

"There are one or two things I must know, Colonel," Barry said after a while, "First, what happens if you *do* find the colt again — find it soon?"

"I bring Lady back, immediately," the moorman said promptly. Barry nodded.

"Then, is she going to be kept as a hawk or will she be a pet?"

The moorman thought for a few moments. "That's a tricky one," he admitted. "Which would you prefer?"

"I would rather she were kept as a hawk."

"Then I promise to see to it, as far as it is

53

possible. You know that there's bound to be some decline in her training — after all the lad has no experience; but I believe that he has a feel for animals and that, really, is the most important thing. Naturally I shall advise him as well as I can, although you know that it's many years since I flew my last hawk. But we'll do our best, I promise."

Barry leaned forward anxiously: "I'm sorry, Colonel, that must have sounded very rude; please forgive me. You've got far more experience than I have and you know it. You shouldn't be so patient with me."

"Nonsense," the moorman said brusquely.

The next morning Barry took the old man a cup of tea at 5 A.M., only to find him already up and dressed. They went out into the grey dawn and walked quietly across the lawn towards the corner where the two hawks were out on their weathering blocks. The Gos appeared to be asleep on her ring perch, her head sunk into her shoulders, her feathers slightly puffed; but Lady was alert and jumped eagerly on to Barry's bare fist. He slipped the hood over her head and she was immediately still. The leash untied, he carried her up the garden and out to the car; she stepped up on to the box cadge and sat quietly, only her head moving slightly to sounds.

"I don't really like the idea of hooding her," Barry said, "but I think it's safer — it's a long run after all. Her crop's full now but don't forget to feed her as soon as you can; and *please* let her have a drink and a bath the moment you arrive, won't you?" The moorman nodded.

"That's what I shall be thinking about myself, so I shan't forget. Don't worry, lad," he added, "everything will be all right. I wouldn't be surprised if you didn't have her home again before long."

Barry shrugged and smiled.

"See how it goes."

The moorman climbed into the driving seat and closed the door quietly. He started the engine then wound his window down.

"I'll give you a ring this evening to confirm our safe arrival."

"That won't be necessary, Colonel, but you could drop me a line once in a while to tell me how she's making out?"

"Of course. Well, Barry, I can't tell you —"

The young man cut him short with a gesture, still smiling slightly.

"No, sir, don't bother, please. Have a good journey. Good-bye."

He turned around and walked back towards the house, looking straight ahead. The moorman watched him for a moment then shook his head once, unhappily, let the handbrake off and drove away.

The next morning, after breakfast, he called for the boy. He had explained his idea to Mrs. Ransome before going north for the little hawk, but had advised her not to mention it to Philip. When the boy came downstairs he looked questioningly at the moorman.

"I've got something for you at home," he replied to the unspoken question. The boy nodded and followed him meekly, his face expressionless.

55

As they walked up the road in the fresh morning the moorman glanced back and saw the mother standing in the open doorway of her home looking after them, one hand up to her face, the other gripping the door-frame as if for support.

The moorman led the boy to the door of the outhouse which had served as a mews for the night, pushed him gently in front and opened the door.

At first the boy saw nothing, standing in the open doorway with all the brilliant day behind him, but his eyes began to adjust to the gloom and he took a step forward. Lady was looking straight at him. Full and confident, her dark eyes shining out from behind the rich yellow cere and the gun-metal beak. He stopped in his tracks and they regarded each other, the two of them; Philip gave a little sigh of wonder and stood as if rooted to the ground. The little hawk bobbed her head a couple of times and began a delicate dance on her perch, stepping from one yellow foot to the other in anticipation. So excellently was she manned that she was totally without fear of strangers and was frankly inviting Philip to take her up; at the same time her manner had that quality of dignity that distinguishes the trained hawk from the pet: There was no air of fawning about her, nor did she scream to him.

The moorman, who had followed the boy in, placed a hand on his shoulder and urged him forward, closer to the perch. The boy stood now about three feet from the bird, and he leaned slightly forward, his arms tight to his sides, looking at her as though his eyes were devouring her.

In the diffused light of the shed her plumage seemed to glow: the rich sienna and darker browns of her upper parts, spotted and barred with black, the warm orange-ochre of her breast-feathers with their streaks and splashes of umber. The long pointed wings were a dark slaty brown and crossed over the tail with its heavy black band tinged with pale grey. Her head was a real falcon's head, a perfect miniature of the swash-buckling peregrine's or the lordly gyrfalcon's, with its black moustachial stripe and the bare yellow skin surrounding the brilliant eyes. For all the softness of her plumage she was a falcon, a sleek little killer, and her hooked beak and black, curved claws were reminders of the fact.

The moorman moved quietly to the perch and untied the leash. He looked at the boy and mo-tioned to him to hold out his hand; the boy was in a trance, so the moorman took the hand, moved it around behind the bird and, operating it as though it were some kind of instrument, placed the jesses* between the pliant fingers and closed the fist. He spoke softly: "Philip, I want you to move your hand so that it touches the back of her legs; keep your fist clenched and move slowly." The boy did so and the hawk stepped neatly backwards and upwards on to the boy's fist. The moorman smiled.

"Right, now take her outside."

The boy moved like a sleepwalker out into the blazing morning, holding the kestrel up in front

---

* The lengths of soft leather attached to a hawk's legs.

of him. As they left the building she looked around busily then roused her feathers in sudden contentment, letting them fall back into a perfection of sleekness.

"Do you know what kind of bird it is?" the moorman asked. The boy looked up at him, turning his pinched, anxious face, his eyes screwed up against the sun.

"A k-k-kestrel," he said quickly. Again the moorman smiled: everything was going just as he had hoped it might.

"It's yours, Philip," he said.

Again the boy looked up at him — just looked this time — then down again at the bird on his fist.

"I'm afraid you can't simply take her away, though; you'll have to learn first how to handle a trained falcon. I'll keep her here for the moment and you must come as often as you can to learn the ropes; it shouldn't take you long and then you'll be able to take her home with you — provided," he added hastily, "your mother agrees," having already obtained her agreement, in fact, but wishing to keep from the boy any hint that the whole operation had been carefully planned.

The boy would have agreed to anything. For the first time since the white colt had disappeared over the sky line he felt his attention focused; felt, as if it were a new experience, his heart beating, his blood running, air entering his lungs; his skin seemed to prickle and suddenly he noticed the soft breeze against his cheek. His eyes filled with tears and he smiled at the hawk on his fist, still gazing benignly at the landscape.

Without thinking he put up his other hand and tickled her under the chin, then stroked her breast-feathers. She lifted her beak as if for more and made soft croaking noises in her throat. The boy looked up:

"W-w-what's her name?"

"Lady," the moorman said.

"Lady," said the boy. "Lady, Lady."

The next few weeks were full ones for the moorman as he took the boy through the rudiments of falconry. He rigged up a screen perch in the disused chicken house in the Ransomes' garden and started with Philip from the very beginning. The boy was quickly absorbed in the task and made steady progress. They spent as many as three or four hours a day with Lady, who positively basked in the attention: It did not bother her how many times she was taken up and put down again while Philip learned to tie the one-handed falconer's knot. If the boy made a particularly noticeable mistake she would bate — that is, she would throw herself off his fist so that she hung by her jesses, flapping her wings in a tantrum — but even this she seemed to do with a patient air, as though it were the only way to teach the boy the right method, as though the whole business of bating was not really her idea at all . . . she was, in short, the perfect beginner's hawk — and Philip was a remarkably apt pupil. Even the moorman was surprised to discover how readily he mastered the necessary skills. A whole new world opened out for the boy as he enjoyed such homely events as the little hawk's daily bath: He laughed delightedly as she thrashed about in the cold water before clambering decorously back to her block, bedraggled and dripping, to dry in the sun.

A sharper, deeper thrill was to see her flying, to watch her learning the wind, investigating the sky for its pattern of air currents, its upward spiralling thermals and sudden down-draughts. Most exciting of all was when she closed her pointed wings and stooped hard and straight at the lure. Here Philip went a little in awe of her: The change was so swift from the soft fluttering companion of the fist to the falling missile that smacked against the lure and the hook-beaked assassin that crouched over it and dared him to take it from her.

During the last week in July the moorman had to go away for a few days; a distant relative had died, a cousin hardly known to him, but he felt family ties strongly and decided to go to the funeral. It was to take place in Essex, so he arranged to stay on in London for a day or two in order to settle some outstanding matters, both business and social. Although he had retired somewhat into the background, leaving Philip a free hand with Lady, he had continued to supervise, gently but firmly, from a distance; faced now with a period of absence that he could not avoid, he worried. It was not that he doubted the boy's ability: He felt that it would be unfair to put Philip into a position where he might be faced, alone, with too big a problem. In the end he telephoned Diana Brookshaw to enlist her aid. He chose Diana because he sensed that she had the same sympathy and understanding for the boy as he had. He did not pause to analyse his decision but went straight to the telephone. Diana herself answered, quite out of breath: "Hallo, Colonel, isn't it a lovely day?"

The moorman smiled down into the receiver, her breathless gaiety was so infectious: "Marvellous. Are you busy?"

"There's enough to do — we're trying to get everything done while the good weather holds. How's Philip getting along with the bird?"

"Splendidly, thank you, and that's what I'm ringing you about, my dear — I want to ask your help if you're not too busy."

"Of course. Fire away."

"Bit too complicated. Can I come and see you this evening — it won't take long."

"Lovely. Come along somewhere around nine — that isn't too late for you?"

"No, no, that'll do fine."

"See you later then, 'bye."

That evening he explained the situation to Diana as they sat in the warm light of the hurricane lamp that lit the living room of the old farmhouse: the electricity supply had been laid on there some years before, but she and John still preferred the lamps with which they had both grown up. Although the moorman had half-expected her to decline because of the amount of work to be done on the farm, Diana agreed gladly to help. It was a simple idea: She was to accompany Philip when he took the kestrel out

61

and was to keep an eye on things generally. In case of any difficulties or doubts she was to telephone the moorman at his hotel — he gave her a piece of paper with his itinerary clearly printed — no matter at what time of day or night.

The moorman had been away for three days and was due to return the following evening. All had gone well: Diana had walked out with the boy each day and had been fascinated by his gentle skill with the little kestrel. Relaxed as he was by his absorption in the kestrel and the calming influence of the surrounding moors he quickly accepted her presence and soon began to respond to her questions. She was genuinely interested by everything that Philip did with the little falcon and could not suppress her curiosity; he answered her with a combination of mime and demonstration.

They neither of them noticed the slight change in Lady's demeanour as they walked along the road towards Brimpts: indeed, only a trained falconer would have noticed, and he might have guessed that she had been overfed. He would have been right. The moorman had written down the exact weights of meat to be fed to her, and had left the chart by the scales so that Philip would not lose it, but that morning his attention had wandered and he had given her far more than her proper ration. He had not noticed her lukewarm welcome and her slightly disgruntled air on being taken up. He did not notice now that she sat listlessly on his fist and failed to look eagerly around her as was her custom. He began to feel the first nagging doubt only when he cast her off into the wind: she rose sluggishly for a few feet and then flapped lazily downwind, looking from side to side for a perch. Philip was puzzled; there was a good fresh breeze and she should have been climbing high above their heads by now. She landed on a wall and sat discontentedly, looking around her as if she had lost something. Philip took a whistle from the bag at his side, raised his gauntleted fist and blew the whistle; he waited, then blew it again and again. From Lady there was no reaction whatever: she was gazing steadily over her shoulder towards the dark mass of Brimpts plantation, a little way off. Diana had not guessed that something was wrong but Philip was frowning anxiously as he took the lure from the bag and started to swing it. When Lady took off from the wall, he felt a sudden sense of relief, but it lasted less than a second — she was flying slowly away from him, across the wind, towards the distant trees. Really frightened now, Philip stuffed the lure back into the bag, already hurrying after the receding kestrel; Diana at last caught his anxiety and ran after him.

"Philip, is something wrong?"

He turned and looked at her once, then hurried on again, his eyes fixed on the slowly flapping wings, hard to see now against the dark mass of the plantation. They saw her perch again in a small tree on the very edge of the wood; she was still there when they arrived at its foot, balancing precariously on the thin twigs at the very top of the tree and managing somehow to convey an impression of ill-temper in her stance. Philip went through the routine again and yet again, but there was no movement. Diana was catching Philip's increasing panic; she noticed that he was very pale and beginning to tremble.

"Why is she like this, Philip?" she asked.

He looked at her and shook his head, his eyes frightened. She felt so helpless, so hampered by her own ignorance, and began to wonder at what point the situation became a crisis and sent her running for the telephone.

They waited there for over two hours before Lady moved again. Philip swung the lure every five or ten minutes but she seemed not to notice their existence. When she did rouse herself it was to fly away over the tree-tops and out of their sight. Philip turned to Diana, his face a mask of horror and disbelief. She caught his hands in her own, afraid for a moment that he might faint. He was shaking uncontrollably now and was making incoherent little sounds in his throat.

"Philip, don't worry — Listen, the Colonel gave me his telephone number in case anything went wrong — I'll go and ring him and he'll tell me what to do. Don't worry. . . ." she pleaded, fighting down her own despair. "Now come along" — an idea struck her — "you can talk to him if you want." But when she started back towards Hexworthy he clung to her hands and pulled against her movement, his eyes saying no, we *must* find her, we *must*.

They walked through the dimness of Brimpts, searching through the tangle of branches for the motionless chestnut and brown shape of Lady. The pine needles deadened their footfalls and the crack of a dry twig breaking beneath Philip's foot made them both jump. Diana heard the clamour of rooks for a full minute before its significance registered. She felt a surge of hope and caught Philip by the hand, leading him towards the sound. By the time they arrived at the tree in which Lady was perching the rooks had gone but other birds had taken over; Diana could distinguish the alarm notes of a blackbird and the harsh scolding of a pair of jays; as they stood beneath the tree a wren appeared and threw its disproportionately powerful voice in with the chorus. With Lady in sight again Philip calmed somewhat, but Diana was faced again with the problem of what to do for the best. She looked at her watch: it was nearly half past six. She made a rapid calculation: three, three and a bit hours daylight . . . leave Philip there to watch Lady, back to the Colonel's house, telephone, then back to Brimpts and risk not being able to find Philip again.

With sudden decision she turned to Philip and said: "Philip, I'm going to telephone the Colonel now — you stay with Lady; I'll come back and find you when I know what to do. All right?" He nodded. When she looked back over her shoulder as she left he was gazing up into the tree looking small and somehow pathetic.

The moorman was halfway through dinner but he came quickly to the telephone. After

Diana had told him what had happened he was silent for a few moments, thinking. When he spoke his voice was crisp and unemotional:

"Have you got pencil and paper?"

She looked around her.

"No."

"You'll find both in the top left-hand drawer of my writing desk."

She fetched note pad and pencil.

"Right."

"Now take this down," he said evenly, "and make sure you get it right."

He spoke slowly, dictating to her phrase by phrase, waiting for her "yes" before going on.

"Tell Philip to tie white handkerchief to lure. When sun is down but before dark, show her lure." He broke off from the dictation to ask her: "Is the tree climbable?"

"No," she replied, "I don't think so."

"Shame. In that case there's only one thing to do if she doesn't come down to the lure — you're not writing this down, are you?"

"No."

"That's good. This is for you: If she's still in that tree when it gets dark, you've got to mark it, *and* how to get to it, clearly enough so that I can follow it in the dark, with a torch."

"But — "

"I'll be leaving inside half an hour. I should arrive home by . . . half past three. We might just do it — " he said, more to himself, then crisply again to Diana:

"I'm sorry you're having all this trouble, my dear, but it's all hands to the pumps now."

"That's all right, Colonel."

"Yes, I know it is; bless you. Now listen, Diana, I've got to be at that tree by the time it starts to get light. Is it far into the wood?"

"Not too far — perhaps a hundred and fifty yards."

"All right; well, I'll leave it to you how you do it, but I must be able to find that tree, or whichever tree she's in. She won't move once it's dark. Think you can do it?"

"I'll think of a way."

"Good lass. You do realise that I shan't be able to manage without your help, do you? It's a terrible thing to ask you, I know."

"Oh, that's all right, I'll ring John."

"Yes. Do it from my place, and you might as well make yourself comfortable there until I get back. Get some sleep. Or would you rather go home and have me collect you there?"

"No, it'll be far easier if I stay here. Colonel, what about Philip — what do I do with him?"

A short silence, during which the pips sounded, then:

"Have a word with his mother and leave it to her — but make sure you tell him that everything's going to be all right — I don't want him worrying himself to death."

"I will."

"I must get cracking. Any more worries?"

"No."

"Good. Till later then."

When she left the moorman's cottage and headed back towards Brimpts she was carrying a tin of white paint and a large brush.

Philip showed Lady the lure with the handkerchief attached as soon as the sun had dropped behind the hill. Interest she showed, but no inclination to act. A few minutes after Philip gave up she roused her feathers and shuffled into a more comfortable position. Half an hour later they could no longer see her.

Diana opened the can of paint and stood irresolutely for a moment, wondering what to do with the lid:

"Oh, the hell with it," she said quietly and threw it away. She painted a broad ring right around the bole of the tree (God knows what the owner will say, she thought — then, irrelevantly, I wonder who the owner is?) and they started back towards the road, Diana putting large splashes of paint on every other tree. Philip seemed to have accepted the situation and had been cheered by the moorman's message of confidence.

When the old man climbed wearily out of his car and walked up to the front door of his cottage it was just after 3 A.M. and Yar Tor was showing dimly against the sky. Diana and Philip were both asleep on the sofa in the study; they had fallen asleep at opposite ends but Philip had fallen across and his head was in her lap; her left arm was thrown protectively across the boy's shoulder. The old man stood looking down at them, his eyes blinking with fatigue; in the light from the reading lamp Diana's face was soft and

68

innocent. He suddenly noticed a smudge of white paint on the side of her nose and a wave of tenderness swept over him so that tears actually started to his eyes. He stood motionless for a few moments, looking at her; then his eyes lifted and saw a dim radiance creeping up the sky. He sighed and bent to wake them.

In the half-light before the dawn Diana's trail was easy to follow and at ten past four they were looking up to where they could just make out Lady's shape against the lightening sky. They settled down to wait for the sun and the woods began to wake all around them. Philip, who had woken hazy with fatigue, slept again on the bed of pine needles and leaf mould. Diana and the moorman talked sporadically; the rest of the time they simply looked around them as the air warmed and the birds' first sleepy chirrups became loud and purposeful.

At half past five Lady stirred. The moorman saw her rouse her feathers and start to look about her. A few minutes later she stretched her legs and wings together in that manner known to falconers as "mantling." He rose quietly to his feet and reached for the bag; Diana too stood up unsteadily, but Philip stayed where he was, curled up on the ground in a deep sleep. The old man unwound the cord wrapped around the lure and began to attach strips of fresh meat to both sides.

"We'll just have to hope she wakes up with an appetite now," he remarked conversationally. He moved away to a clearing about thirty yards from the tree and peered up to make sure that Lady would have a clear field of vision from where she

69

perched. Satisfied, he shook the lure out and began to swing it cautiously, careful not to hit any of the neighbouring trees. Fortunately the little falcon's night in the open air had put a sharp edge to her morning hunger; as soon as she saw the lure she froze, her eyes fixed on it unblinkingly; the next second she took off and hurtled down towards it. The moorman, seeing her coming, let the lure fall to the ground and stood quite still. Lady landed on it with a thud and crouched over it, her wings spread, her beak half-open; soon, however, she put her head down and began to eat, tearing voraciously at the lean steak. The moorman gave her half a minute and then began making in to her, crouching low and moving slowly and quietly. At last he knelt within reach of her. As he moved his hand almost imperceptibly towards the trailing jesses she turned her head sharply and crouched as if ready to spring. The old man held his breath and for a few seconds they presented a tableau in arrested motion, but Lady turned back to her meat and he was able to take up the jesses with a silent prayer of thanksgiving. Philip woke so numb with fatigue that he hardly seemed to register her recapture. He fell asleep again in the moorman's car during the four minute drive back to Hexworthy and slept on well into the morning.

CHAPTER V

AUGUST STILLED THE BREEZES, frightened away the clouds; the sun held dominion. Rains came, fell vertical and heavy, then left, and the moor steamed. The bilberries hung in brilliant clusters, weighing down the thin stems that supported them. Sudden fires swept the moor as children and fools set fire to the heath, exercising the ancient right of "swaling" supposed to have been conferred under charter by King John. In fact the right, if there is one, is possessed by only a few, but each year conflagrations start all over the moor, eating away the beneficial heather and giving immediate access to the fast-spreading and pernicious bracken. Already the moor was scarred and striped by blackened wastelands.

Towards the end of the first week of the month the barometer began to slide. The air became still and heavy. Great piled ranges of cumulo-nimbus clouds waited, grumbling, at the boundaries of the moor, never overhead yet always massively visible. "It's coming," they all said, nodding their heads sagely, "it's coming all right."

On the afternoon of the second day the storm still had not broken. The moorman decided not to go far from home, so he wandered about his garden seeking employment. He was trimming a hedge down with a bill-hook when he heard a sound from the direction of the open moor. He straightened up, wiping the sweat from his forehead with the back of his hedging glove and peered out through the thickening air to trace its source. Then he saw the boy two hundred yards away, running madly towards him. As the tiny figure approached and elongated he saw something bouncing and jolting on the boy's arm — saw wings flapping desperately, the spread tail jerking to maintain a kind of balance.

He threw the bill-hook to the ground, savagely. "For God's sake!" he shouted and hurried towards the moor gate, pulling off his gloves as he went. He closed the gate behind him and turned: The boy was nearly up to him; he could see the eyes wide in the pale face, the open mouth; he could hear the boy's incoherent, gasping shouts. He looked again at the kestrel: She was almost flying but was being jarred and jolted by the captive jesses as the boy's arm flailed. At this appalling treatment to the falcon the old man's blood boiled; he felt a surge of terrible anger rise in his throat. He stood erect, unconsciously at the position of attention: his arms held close to his sides, his thumbs against the side seams of his filthy

72

corduroy trousers. He was almost blind with fury.

The boy arrived in front of him, stumbling, his mouth working, his eyes staring dementedly. Something snapped in the old man's head — he fought to prevent himself from striking the boy where he stood. Instead he roared, in terrible anger: "What the hell do you mean by this, boy!"

Philip froze, aghast. "Straighten yourself up! Go on, straighten up!" His mouth hanging open, his chest heaving as he fought for breath, the boy did so. The moorman pointed a trembling finger at him.

"Now look at that! Look at it, boy! What the bloody hell do you mean by it!"

Philip had seen the white colt in a group of ponies; he had gone after it but they were moving away from him faster than he could follow. Desperate at the thought of losing it yet again he had turned and headed for the moorman's cottage. In his desperation he had run blindly, forgetting everything — even the little hawk on his fist. Now, stunned by the anger in the old man's voice, the boy did as he was told, looking down at his gauntleted fist as if he had never seen it before. The little hawk was bating, hanging upside-down by her jesses from his tight clenched fist, her wings flapping feebly in terror and pain. Like someone sleep walking, the boy put his free hand beneath her and lifted her back on to his fist, looking at her with incredulous eyes. She crouched on the fist, her eyes opaque with distress, her beak gaping. The old man saw two broken primaries on her left wing and he had to close his eyes and clench his teeth to stop his wrath from choking him. Every muscle tense and straining he reached out for the hawk. Between his teeth he hissed: "All right. Give her to me!"

A flicker of intelligence stirred in the boy's dazed eyes. Without handing over the hawk he suddenly pointed out towards the moor, looking the old man full in the eyes. "Come on, boy, give her to me. Quickly." He reached out and forced the boy's nerveless fingers apart, taking first the jesses and then the pathetic creature by force. The boy's eyes were still upon him. Through his anger he suddenly saw the plea in the boy's staring eyes, but his anger was such that it was in control of him and he shouted at the boy, choking his words: "Now get out of here!"

He saw the boy's face begin to crumble. He saw the tears start. He saw the mouth work frantically, and suddenly words emerged like broken stones: "B-but . . . our . . . th-the pony . . . my . . . my . . ."

He knew what he was doing, the old man; he felt the injustice, the conscious cruelty of it; but he had never been able to stand the sight of an animal suffering at the hands of a human being, and the kestrel's terror and pain had disturbed him beyond reason and charity.

"Get out! Get away, go on! And don't you ever come near this hawk again or I'll beat the living daylights out of you!"

The boy stood for fully ten seconds, swaying,

then his face seemed to fall into little pieces. He turned away and rested his hand on the stone wall for a moment, his body twisted and still. He gave a low, wordless cry that was an expression of the purest disbelief and horror, and ran away, stumbling, his hands fluttering like shattered white moths.

The old man strode towards the shed wherein Lady has passed her first night. As he went he muttered over and over "Christ, oh Christ, oh Christ, oh Christ . . ." Moving like a clockwork toy, he put the crazed and exhausted hawk into the neutral darkness of the blacked-out shed. His hands were gentle with her, yet trembling, hurrying to put her kindly on to the perch, to tie the difficult knot, hurrying to go out and close the door, leaving her to who knows what dreams of flapping screaming terror in the darkness.

He stood outside the shed for a moment in the low, threatening afternoon, distressed and shaking, then he went towards his car as a line of action flashed into his thoughts: Now find the pony. Find the pony. Quickly.

The old car bounced and rolled as the moorman drove it mercilessly through the village, over the hump-backed bridge across the Dart and out towards Dartmeet. The sky was low and threatening; peering up, the old man could see the jagged tooth of Yar Tor grazing the clouds. Murmurs of distant thunder trembled in the hazy air. He did not know where the boy had seen the colt, only the direction whence he had come, so he slowed down and began searching the parts of the moor visible from the road as they drifted past in a parallax of changing colours. But the moors seemed to be deserted. Sheep there were, like ragged grey-white rocks, standing singly or in small flocks; but only an isolated pony or two, small family groups, specks in the middle distance. He turned left towards Two Bridges and searched carefully along the valley to the left and the rising ground to the right. Then back the way he had come, through Hexworthy and out on the Holne road. His depression deepened as the search continued unsuccessful. At last he gave up and drove morosely back towards Hexworthy. A mile out, he saw a small gnomelike figure shuffling bow-leggedly at a great pace towards the village and recognised old Reg. In his despondency he did not want to talk to the sharp old fellow, so he did not slacken speed; but as he approached Reg turned, recognised the car and started to wave wildly. The moorman braked sharply, cursing under his breath. He wound down the window and the hooked nose and blue eyes of the old man appeared, framed by the collar of the overcoat he wore even on the hottest day. The moorman opened his mouth to speak but the old man gabbled excitedly: "You seen'un then, Cunnel?"

"Seen whom?"

"Why, thiccy pawny!"

The moorman caught on. He gripped the wheel. "Where is he, Reg?"

"He'm up-over Cumston way. I were rushin' doan to tell 'ee."

"Climb in then, come on!"

Reg bundled into the passenger seat and sat gripping the windscreen ledge with both hands, pulling himself forward so that he could see out as the old Ford hurtled back down the hill, over the stream and up the long slope towards Combestone Tor. They left the car off the road and half ran across the close cropped turf around the great pile of granite, the little old man making a great puffing and muttering as he followed in the moorman's wake. They cleared the side of the tor and the whole rolling expanse of the moor lay before them, shining beneath the heavy purple-brown sky. Old Reg came up beside the moorman and pointed tremblingly down into the nearest depression.

"He were doan there, Cunnel, wi' six or seven other pawnies."

The moorman swept the landscape methodically, sector by sector: the ubiquitous sheep, again a few sparse groups of ponies, but no flash of white from the patchwork of purple, grey, russet and umber, green and ochre that shimmered breathlessly as if awaiting something.

"They may be hidden in that dead ground there — come on, Reg!"

And he strode off into the heather, the breathless old man scuttling after him, his cheeks scarlet with exertion, his almost toothless mouth working, a drip suspended precariously at the tip of his eaglelike nose. But they were not in the dead ground that lay below the brow of Combestone Tor. As they stood there, the moorman again felt the sense of a depression too deep to

77

fathom, a cold arid hopelessness. They turned and began the long difficult walk across the clitter-strewn slope towards the road; as they did so, the storm finally broke. There were a few premonitory rolls of thunder and then the whole sky seemed to detonate. The two old men stood for a minute or two, awed by the play of lightning through the tumbled clouds above them; then they saw the rain marching down towards them like a great grey wall of water. They rushed forward precipitately, but it was a futile gesture. The rain overtook them and swallowed them as though they were two scurrying insects. By the time they reached the car they were as wet as though they had been swimming in their clothes. On their way back they steamed and the moorman had to wipe the inside of the windscreen when it became misted. Reg spoke only once:

"I seed 'un there, Cunnel."

"I know you did, Reg. We'll find him, don't you worry."

"Yass, I seed 'un."

The moorman drove him back to Sherberton. When the old man had clambered out he turned and thrust his ancient pixie face back inside the car, his blue eyes peering earnestly at the moorman from beneath his bedraggled bushes of eyebrows.

"If yew want me to come along an' help 'ee, midear, when yew gaw lookin' for thiccy pawny, do 'ee tell me then, woan't 'ee?"

"Thank you, Reg. I'll be going again tomorrow morning, about seven. Will that be too early?"

78

"Naw, midear, I can't lay abed. John wan't mind me goin' along with 'ee."

The moorman sat and watched the tatterdemalion figure scuttling away through the mud of the farmyard towards the great pile of the old house, built like a tor itself, of grey moorstone.

The rain was a steady drizzle now that the storm's passion was spent, and as the moorman drove through it his heart sank within him at the thought of what he now must do. Mrs. Ransome greeted him anxiously: "Oh, Colonel, come in out of the rain."

He stepped inside and stood in the hall while she closed the front door. She spoke as if out of breath:

"I'm so glad you've come — I don't know what's wrong with Philip, he's in a terrible state. I've called the doctor. He came in — oh, before the rain started — deathly pale and making strange noises — he ran straight past me — " She stopped abruptly when she saw his expression.

"Why, Colonel, what's wrong?"

An expression of pain and distaste on his face, the moorman answered: "It was my fault, Mrs. Ransome."

"Your fault? But how on earth — "

"I shouted at him, Mrs. Ransome. He made me — I lost my temper and shouted at him."

She stood there trying to grasp what he had said, her eyes burning fever-bright, different emotions flickering across her features. At last she said: "You *what?*"

He said once again, as if in expiation: "I shouted at him. It's my fault."

"Then there's nothing else . . ."

"No, there's nothing else wrong with him. Just that."

"But . . ." She fell silent. He stood, waiting for her to understand. He could hear the drops of water falling from his clothes to the floor. She spoke again, but this time it was with another voice: a voice trembling with barely suppressed anger: "You *shouted* at him?"

He nodded. Standing there awkwardly. Her indignation burst out finally, "But no one has ever shouted at him. Why did you have to?" Her face was suffused. She was a mother defending her young one, transformed.

"I'm sorry, Mrs. Ransome."

"I'll bet you're sorry! The damage you've done — "

"I'll try to put it right," he said quietly.

"Put it right! Put it right, you say! What do you think we've been trying to do for years and years?"

He went on, speaking quietly but more firmly now: "Mrs. Ransome, you must listen to me a moment."

She stood before him, her big body braced, her fists clenched, her eyes blazing.

"The pony is back. At least, he's not far away. I'm going to find him: I must. It's our only chance of mending the damage. Please cooperate with me, for the boy's sake."

"You should have thought of him earlier!" she said, but her voice had lost its ring of righteousness, and uncertainty was creeping back.

"I know," he said simply, "and now I want to

80

do what I can to put things right. Will you be ready to help if I find the pony?"

She looked at him a few moments longer, then she started to cry. She covered her face with her big red hands and cried with terrible shuddering sobs. He stood, waiting, but she turned abruptly and ran down the hall and through a doorway. He let himself out of the house and drove himself home.

After he had changed into dry clothes he prepared to tackle the next problem. On arriving back at the house he had taken some kidney from the refrigerator and put it into warm water to soften. Now he cut it into small squares and put them into his falconer's bag. Then he took down his spare gauntlet from its nail and went out into the garden. The rain was still falling, but a light breeze had got up and now its steady rushing was punctuated by miniature squalls and the air was much cooler. So abstracted was the old man that he almost forgot the task ahead of him with the fear-crazed kestrel, almost thought that he was going out to feed her in the normal way. He came to when he opened the shed door.

After frozen seconds of button-eyed, paralysed fear, she bated away from him. Not feebly, as she had done when she had hung exhausted from the boy's fist, but with renewed strength, with power, with a blind determination to escape she beat her wings, flailing them against the hessian that hung below the perch, her head strained back, her beak gaping.

A though flashed through the old man's mind: That's a wild hawk. He pulled out a wooden box from the corner and sat down heavily, then put his head in his hands and surrendered to weariness and despair. What a day, his thoughts went. What a day. What a day. What a day. The rain drummed wildly on the roof and against the wooden walls of the shed; the wind moaned and whispered as it blew up out of desolation and licked across the pitiful little spreading blots of civilisation and comfort that crouched in the lap of the old moor. The only other sound was the steady, frantic flapping of beautiful, once-tame wings.

The air was fresh and clear, the clouds high. As the moorman strode through the heather, droplets of pure water scattered, catching the early sun in minute rainbows. The whole landscape was glowing with new subtleties of colour.

A distant shout brought the old man's head up like a stag's. It came again, thin and brittle. His heart lifted and he changed direction towards it, taking great strides through the heather, leaping and stumbling across the clitter. It came a third time, recognisable this time: "Cunnel!"

The next moment Reg came into view, leaping and gesticulating. Far beyond him the moorman saw a group of ponies, and amongst them a flash of white. His eyes lifted involuntarily for a second as he said "Thank God." The sky was bland.

But they could not catch the white colt. The moorman had taken a halter and bread crusts, but they could not get within twenty yards of it. In spite of all his patient efforts to approach, in spite of Reg's perspiring, vehemently cursing attempts to herd it away from its companions, it would not be caught. So it was that for the second time in twenty-four hours the moorman found himself standing at the Ransomes' front door.

Mrs. Ransome was subdued and pale. She asked him in politely and took him into the living-room. It was Saturday and her husband was sitting in his dressing gown reading a newspaper. He jumped to his feet and they shook hands, embarrassed. The moorman broached the subject without preamble.

"I've found the pony, not far from here, but I can't catch it. I know that Philip won't want to see me, but if I tell him that we have found his pony I'm sure he will come and catch it; then we can bring it back and I'll put it in my paddock — you know, the one behind my cottage." Mrs. Ransome looked anxiously at her husband.

"I don't know . . ." she said, hesitating. Her husband explained:

"Philip was in rather bad shape last night and we had to get the doctor again. He gave him a sedative."

The moorman closed his eyes for a moment as the boy's incoherent cry rang in his mind, then opened them again and went on: "I really do think that this is sufficiently important to warrant waking him. If he can get his pony back he'll have a much better chance, surely."

"But he was getting on fine with Lady," said Mrs. Ransome. "Is the pony so important?"

83

"I'm afraid that Lady will be no use to anyone for quite a long time, Mrs. Ransome."

"Oh," she said, and perhaps began to understand. Before she could say any more the moorman said: "Look, would you go and explain the position to Philip. Tell him I've got halter and food for the pony and the car is outside. It's only a mile away, or a little more."

Mrs. Ransome made up her mind. "I'll go and tell him," she said and left the room. The moorman turned to her husband, still standing awkwardly in his dressing gown, still holding the opened newspaper, trailing in his left hand.

"The pony can stay in my paddock for now while we work things out," he said. "Apart from certain complications regarding ownership and so on, I'd like to discuss the whole situation with you and your wife. May I come over and see you some evening—or an even better idea: come over and see me." He thought for a moment then went on: "Look, when Philip's safely in bed tomorrow night, come over and have a drink, the two of you. Will you?" The smaller, balding man cleared his throat nervously.

"Yes. Yes, thank you very much. I'll talk to my wife about it. It sounds very nice."

"Good. I'll be off, then. No, don't see me out, I know the way."

Ten minutes later Philip came out of the door and walked down the path to the car, blinking in the bright sunlight. Old Reg had moved into the back, and the boy climbed into the passenger seat without a word, looking straight ahead. The moorman was appalled at the damage that showed on his face: It seemed half its former size and had an old, haunted look about it.

Old Reg knew about Philip. Everyone knew. In his embarrassment and concern he kept up a staccato monologue meant to cheer the boy up, but Philip sat looking out of the side window, away from the moorman, only his eyes moving.

The colt was still where they had left it. They stopped on the brow of the hill as the group of ponies came into view. The moorman observed the boy closely. As he stood looking intently at the colt, he seemed to breathe more deeply. The moorman handed him the halter; the boy took it without a word and walked away from them towards the distant group. Old Reg started forward to follow but the moorman laid a restraining hand on his arm.

"No, Reg, not this time, old lad. Let the boy go."

They stood silently and watched as the boy's figure receded; they saw the ponies look up: first one, then the rest, and move away — all but one who stood mildly regarding the approaching figure. There was no joyful reunion, no neigh of recognition; it was all quite ordinary. The boy just walked up to the white colt holding the halter out before him and the colt seemed to put its head quietly into the noseband and allow the boy to buckle it. It was all over.

As the boy led the pony towards them the two men walked to meet him. The moorman even found himself hoping that the recapture of the pony might have wrought a sudden change in the boy, a sort of miraculous cure; as they converged he found himself almost believing that Philip would greet him and laugh with pleasure, but the boy was still white-faced and looked away when the moorman spoke.

"Take him to the paddock behind my house, Philip. He'll be safe there while we sort things out."

The boy set off immediately, the colt walking behind him as though it had grown old in service.

As they walked back to the car old Reg was shaking his head and muttering under his breath.

"What is it, Reg?" the moorman asked.

"Thiccy boy — 'tis a bliddy shame, I reckon, a bliddy shame."

The moorman understood and said no more; Old Reg went on muttering all the way back to the car and then all the way to the moorman's cottage, where they came to a halt. The moorman spoke: "Just hang on a moment while I fetch something, Reg, then I'll drive you back home." He returned with something wrapped in paper, which he put on to the back seat, and drove on to Sherberton. When they had arrived and old Reg was getting out, he reached across for the paper-wrapped object and handed it out to the old man.

"I want you to have that, Reg, for all you've done. No arguments now."

The old man knew that it was Johnny Walker by its shape and his red face split into a thousand lines of pleasure and excitement. "Thankee, thankee, Cunnel. You'm a bliddy fine man, mi-dear!"

He stood in the road watching the moorman

86

out of sight, holding on to the precious bottle with both hands, chuckling and whispering to himself. Then suddenly his expression changed: A furtive look appeared on his face. He glanced quickly to right and left, then stuffed the bottle deep into the layers of clothing over his birdlike chest. Hunched and secretive, he tiptoed through the gate and across the yard, shooting fierce looks into every shadow and around every corner; his blue eyes seeming to hide in turn behind the enormously hooked nose. Both arms wrapped tightly around the telltale lump in his overcoat, he ran the last few yards to safety with his caracteristic high-kneed scuttle. Half an hour later the Johnny Walker bottle was lying horizontally inside the lining of his mattress, and the old man himself was tackling the day's work with a snap and vigour that promised a good thirst later in the day.

The moorman, as he drove round the hairpin bends above the Forest Inn, wondered why he felt so tired all of a sudden.

He ate a hurried lunch and tried to rest but it was no good; as he sat in his armchair he felt stifled, the walls leaned in, the furniture crowded him, the very air was hostile. He felt, or rather he sensed great cracks appearing in his serenity and seemed to hear the scratching of ancient fears and old pains, remembered well from long ago. He poured himself a drink with unsteady hands and drank half of it, pulling a face as the raw spirits tore at his throat. Still holding the glass he walked over to the window and looked out over the moor with unseeing eyes.

"I didn't want to be involved," he said suddenly and savagely. "How did I get involved?" His eyes moved blindly across the horizon as if looking for an answer, but none came. "Bloody fool," he said. He raised the glass to his mouth, then stopped and looked at it in disgust. He shuddered violently and slammed it down on the window-ledge, spilling some of the whisky so that it lay vividly on the white paint-work, already gathering a delicate film of dust. But the old man had gone.

Driving fast along the good road that leads to Two Bridges, he put his driving window down and let the wind of his passage envelop him, warm and blustering. The storm had washed the moor of its dust and now the air sparkled. Larks hung in the sky and their trilling song drifted down like petals; so real, so tangible that the old man had the impression that he was driving through it as it fell, a soft silver rainfall of lark-song.

He had gone straight over the T-junction towards Princetown before he realised where he was going. As soon as he knew, he felt himself calm a little: He felt in anticipation the ancient silence of the place that was drawing him, like a lodestone, towards its heart.

Opposite the Two Bridges Hotel he slowed down and then pulled in to a gateway, off the road. As he switched the ignition off and the old motor hiccupped into silence, the babbling of running water flooded his senses, spreading over the inflamed surface of his soul like a cool balm. Yet there was still something hot and hard and angry at the centre of him that caught at his breathing and pressed against his diaphragm. He went through the gate and started to follow the track that ran alongside a wall of moorstone curving massively up the gentle slope towards the moor beyond. He walked fast, with an insectlike regularity to his strides, mechanically, his head bent, his forehead creased in a frown. Suddenly a sharp pain seared across his ribs like a red-hot knife. He staggered and almost fell against the wall, pressing one hand hard against his chest, his eyes closed while the pain burned and then opened as it passed as suddenly as it had come. His face was off-white with a tinge of grey and beads of sweat were breaking out on his forehead. He relaxed, but still leaned back against the wall. Fumbling in the pocket of his old jacket he pulled out a handkerchief and wiped his face carefully. For a little while then he remained still, quite still, while his breathing became normal and the colour crept back into his face. Finally he stood upright again, but there was no recurrence of the pain. As he walked on he spoke silently to his legs: "Easy, easy now; take it easy, no hurry; easy — " It did not occur to him to turn back.

The skyline on his right hand rose as the valley fell away on his left. Even though he was climbing steadily, higher and higher above the white-dashed river below him, the broken horizon on his right continued to recede. The valley, the whole expanse, seemed to be opening out, becoming

89

wider; and as the landscape grew, so the old man seemed to shrink, until he felt himself an insect on a vast plain moving with unbelievable slowness towards a horizon at which he would never arrive.

The track become a memory. The old man moved across the enormous grey-clittered slope beneath Longaford Tor. He had no pain now, only a weak fluttering against his heart.

Where am I going? he thought, walking here in the middle of nowhere. What am I seeking? What is so important that I must find it? Tell me, he said to the moor around him. He felt a sudden pressure inside his forehead and paused in wonder as tears started sharply in his eyes, threatened, but did not fall. "Dotage" flashed across his mind; I am getting old, this is senility . . . decay. No! his mind shouted fiercely, No and no! He clenched his fists, and his eyes yearned towards the shimmering horizon. My youth was a dream! he shouted silently, nothing but a dream! He walked on again, blindly. A grey smudge showed dimly round the curve of the valley where it fell towards the Dart. It was his goal, his desired end; it was where he hoped peace would be waiting for him. His mind was drowning in memories, sensual and sharp, like light reflected off broken water, refracted spectrally through decay. No! his mind shouted fiercely, No and no! blown spray . . . he reached out for something to grip, for something solid. Words came into his mind. Solid words like carved stone, unassailable words, heavy and comforting . . . *Hunc non ruricolae Panes . . . Panes, Panes . . . Hunc non . . .*

He felt himself steadying, finding his balance. Grimly he sought to order the words, to set them in their place, anything . . . he spoke out loud:

"Lucus erat longo nunquam violatus ab aevo,
Obscurum cingens connexis aera ramis —"

Was that madness? Imbecility? Is it going to happen —

"Et gelidas alte summotis solibus umbras."

Better, calmer, easier now. But what was it? Quietly, what was it now? All of a sudden I was no longer I, but all my years together dying and being born, all together, sinking down and down —

Hunc non ruricolae Panes, nemorumque potentes
Silvani Nymphae que tenent —"

The first stunted trees seemed to grow up out of the moor as he approached, grey and soft and indistinct in their peculiar mistlike silence, brooding —

"Sed barbara ritu Sacra Deum, structae sacris feralibus arae
Omnis et humanis lustrata cruoribus arbos."

The old man spoke the last terrible lines in a voice that rang with a kind of triumph . . . the words were so strong, so stark.

The wood lay before him . . . Wistman's Wood. Ancient and still, crouching close to the hillside. He picked his way carefully now over the difficult ground; his mind, soothed somehow by Lucan's glowering verse, was absorbed entirely in the effort of making progress over the deep-piled boulders. Once there had been mountains: mountains of granite standing grey and gaunt against the rain-bearing westerly winds. But the winds had weathered the granite over aeons of time; the rains had beaten against the exposed rock-faces, seeking out every crack, every fault, every fissure; the frosts had come, sharp and deadly, and great slabs of granite had fallen away from the mountains, broken off with an echoing report by the intolerable pressure of the moisture expanding as it froze. Now the skeletons of the mountains remained, like decaying stumps of teeth, while all around them lay the "clitter", the detritus of hundreds of thousands of years of erosion.

Wistman's Wood grows out of clitter. The weird stunted oaks grow tortuously out from amongst the piled boulders as if trying to escape. Few are more than twelve feet high, many are less, yet they are hundreds of years old. The soil is too poor, the rocks too many and too tumbled, so the trees writhe and twist as they crouch, and lock and interlock incestuously. While the soil that lies in the crevices is poor, the air is dank and rich with moisture; mosses and lichens luxuriate, staining the rocks over and over, maculating the writhing trunks with the myriad colours of decomposition; fragile ferns grow; pale, fleshy parasites cling to the limbs, sucking the slow sap with hollow tongues. Although the Dart lisps and tumbles in the valley below, there is a muffled silence in the wood, and no birds sing there.

The moorman stood a little above the enchanted grove gazing down into the silent depths, breathing in its atmosphere of mystery and antiquity. It is popularly supposed to have been held sacred by the Druids. There is an undeniable air of something atavistic; something deep and old; the wood breathes with an ancient evil.

Sanity returned. The old man stood motionless, gazing down towards the river over the dwarf trees, breathing in the sweet air as it drifted down from the high blanket moors to the north. He had been stretched by the emotional exertions of the preceding few days and his heart's sudden frightening rebellion had momentarily upset the fine balance of his mind: He had teetered over a great darkness and had recovered.

I am an old man, he thought, and he smiled briefly; but he did not fully believe it. He sat down where he could lean back and rest against a rounded boulder; with his eyes unfocused towards the far horizon he fumbled for and filled his pipe, then sat puffing at it, the gentle breeze causing the burning tobacco to glow white. He sat looking out across the wide valley. On the opposite slope, towards Bairdown, he could see sheep grazing, almost indistinguishable from the rocks. Clouds drifted easily up the sky, against the current of the river below. Somewhere a curlew cried, and the old man turned his head towards the sound, his lips moving:

> O curlew, cry no more in the air,
> Or only to the waters in the West . . .

Always these three things together, the cry of the curlew, Yeat's passionate words and the ineffable loneliness, the taste of all sorrow that comes down off the high desolate moors with the unhurrying wind: all the essence of the moors expressed in one forlorn cry.

Walking back towards his car, much later, he no longer feared the weeks ahead.

There was a rather uncomfortable meeting that evening at the moorman's cottage. He had wanted to explain so much — having found that he could talk easily with Mrs. Ransome — but the presence of her husband seemed to weave a spell of nervousness about the whole proceedings. She, for her part, had wanted to apologise to the moorman for her outburst, but this too was still-born. This strange grey man, her husband, seemed to create an atmosphere of awkwardness like an aura about him, so that normally relaxed people caught within this sphere of influence, became nervous too. An excellent man at his job, he had a gift for clearly stating a legal situation with all its contingencies and implications logically marshalled and lucidly expressed. When dealing with the ramifications of the law he felt a sense of power, he seemed to come alive; the great law books in his office were not allowed their hallowed impartiality: they were drawn into his legal struggles, forced to commit themselves friend or foe, to join him and back him or take the consequences. A favourable precedent would send him impetuously forward from beachhead to advance positions, his cheeks flushed, his eyes bright, poised for victory. Within the nonhuman context of law he could be truly himself; it was only humanness that he feared. He was afraid of meeting people anywhere except in his office or the law-courts, discussing anything personal with anyone, his wife and his son, in ascending order. With his wife he had found a way of living that suited them both quite well; occasional meetings with his son disturbed him profoundly and he avoided contact with the boy. Philip, as a consequence, was hardly aware of his father.

The moorman, finding that he could not speak as freely as he had anticipated, no longer tried to explain matters, but confined himself to business. This was quite clearly defined and rather pressing: the ownership of the white colt. Contary to popular belief there are no wild ponies on Dartmoor. Every pony has a brand or an identification mark somewhere. That morning the moorman had glanced quickly over the colt, looking for a brand: He had seen one showing faintly under the coat on the side of the shoulder, just above the elbow. It was not a local one and was in fact unfamiliar to him. He explained to the boy's parents that the matter could not be allowed to rest as it was; that it amounted to stealing, in fact; that the pony's owner had to be traced and some kind of understanding arrived at; and that he, the moorman, was prepared to do all of this for them. What he still had not told them as they took their leave was that he intended buying the colt and presenting it to the boy.

CHAPTER VI

Reclaiming is the name given by falconers to the task ahead of the moorman. "Manning," that is to say, taming a wild falcon so that she will sit relaxed and confident on the fist, is one thing. Reclaiming a hawk which has been frightened or ill-used is another thing altogether. The old man tackled it with patience and fortitude, returning over and over to the very beginning; gradually expunging with every soft word, every titbit gently given, the nightmare within the little falcon's head. Time and again she would appear to have recovered her confidence, sitting contentedly on his fist, when a sound or a movement would produce yet another panic-stricken bate. So back again to the beginning, and nothing but kindness, gentleness, patience, and time: hour after hour in her presence, rebuilding her confidence. If the old man had lacked patience when he had shouted at the boy, he was surely atoning for it now.

Meanwhile the colt was beginning its new role of domesticity in the paddock behind the moorman's cottage. It was fat and content, its coat shining with a limpid whiteness that made it visible for miles in the clear sunlight. The moorman would see the boy daily as he came to lead the pony out on to the moor, but there was no contact between them. If they passed close by each other the boy would look away, his face twisted and pale. The old man realised that it was going to be a slow business, so he reapplied himself to the reclamation of the hawk.

The boy, too, had a problem. From his first inchoate possessiveness towards the colt a more practical desire had precipitated: to ride it. In characteristic fashion he read a book on riding and his head was full of disjointed instructions and half-remembered fragments of information, but in no way could he apply these to the actual physical problem ahead of him. All his life he had seen local farmers on their ponies, herding sheep or riding after hounds, without ever questioning the miracle that had set them on their mounts. Perhaps he had half imagined a sort of rustic necromancy, a laying-on of hands, but he had never brought this dim idea under the light of inspection until he read the book about riding. This confused him even more — naturally, since it was intended to help those trying to get more out of a trained horse. Although he went over and over certain parts of it, he never really understood; he sought in vain some paragraph, some sentence even, which would help him cross the enormous distance between their dual existence

and the centaur he desired to be. So he would sit
by the hour in his room, before going to bed, in
a sort of trance, stroking or simply touching the
waiting bridle. In his mind he was trying to
imagine himself into the pony's skin, into its
blood and muscle, so that he could understand
how it would react to him, to the sudden weight
and grip behind the withers. His eyes closed, his
breathing quick and shallow, he would tremble
within the smooth white coat and stare through
those pale blue eyes at his own approaching form,
shivering with apprehension at the hovering
miracle; then start, leap, plunge, gallop at the
sun, heart frozen by the clawing fear on his back
. . . and he would wake, eyes staring, hands
clutching convulsively, his heart racing, so real
had been the dream.

Yet not a dream; rather a kind of knowledge
based on intuition that has slipped down out of
our minds. The moorman knew about it and
recognised it in the boy.

So the boy threw himself again and again into
this anoetic dream, always fingering the bridle or
a part of the saddle as a sort of link or association
with the animal, and learned. . . .

But it was the halter, not the bridle, that Philip
carried over his shoulder when he went to the
paddock one morning. When he had finally
decided to take the first fateful step, the steel of
the bit had seemed too hard, too bright, too unfor-
giving; with his eyes shut, within the animal's

dark mind, the bit had burnt and terrified his grass-soft mouth and now he was himself afraid of it and had hidden it away from sight. The halter, instead, seemed gentle and pliable, and its rope and canvas felt more like flesh than the stiff leather of the bridle.

He leaned over the gate and watched the colt as it grazed, his diaphragm taut with excitement, his knuckles white as he gripped the top bar of the gate. When he had calmed a little he climbed over the gate and walked towards the pony. It lifted its head and regarded him lazily, then ceased to chew the grass still hanging from its mouth when it saw the halter. It sniffed at it, ears pricked in interest, then snorted and started chewing again as the boy rubbed its neck and ears. He slipped the halter over the pony's head and led it to the shelter in the corner of the field.

This shelter was of simple construction: three sides of wood, a sloping, corrugated iron roof and an open front. It was designed to provide shelter from the prevailing winds, and in a severe spell straw could be shaken down to provide a warm bed. Philip took the pony inside and tied it to an iron ring attached to the back wall; the colt began pulling at some old hay left in the rack and paid no attention whatsoever to the boy as he ran his hands over its back and loins, not even when he pressed carefully down just back of the withers. Encouraged, the boy went further. Standing beside the colt, he leaned over it and let his weight rest across its back: the colt hardly seemed aware of him. Now the boy fetched an old bale of straw from the corner of the shelter and lugged it into position at the pony's side. Moving slowly and talking all the while, he stepped up on to it and stood leaning forward stroking the white back below him: a suspicious look from one shadow-dimmed blue eye and a quick exhalation of breath, but no more, and again the colt was pulling at the hay. For a long time the boy stood on the bale looking down at the colt. Its whole appearance had changed with the boy's new viewpoint: the neck seemed longer, the shoulder narrower and the swell of the rib-cage infinitely wider than from the ground. He stared fascinated at that lowest part of the back where hour after hour he had imagined himself seated, feeling the power of the colt's life surging through his legs. After what seemed to be hours of immobility he leaned across the waiting back and slid his right leg across to the far side; a moment of hesitation, then he slid down to a sitting position and sat tensely, holding the thick mane with both hands. Nothing. The colt stood motionless yet relaxed. The boy too began to relax; he let go of the mane and patted the neck beneath, then started stroking the soft coat all around where he sat. The pony's warmth began to come through his jeans and with it a sense of exaltation; huge vistas opened up before him: The whole moor was his to gallop over, the wind rushed at his face and tangled in his hair, he could hear the hooves drumming beneath him as his body swung and surged at one with the white power beneath him. So the boy dreamed, sitting on the motionless white pony in the shade of the lean-to shelter through the warmth of the morning.

The dream ebbed, reality flowed, he was again aware of his surroundings. Still moving with infinite care he felt for the straw bale with his left foot, then swung his right leg over the pony's back and off. Now he pulled the bale away, untied the halter and led the colt out into the sunshine. He took it to the most level part of the field and prepared for the second step. Again he patted and stroked, pressed and leaned; again the pony took no notice, grazing unconcernedly. Without the assistance of the bale he had to give a little jump but he did so without mishap and finally lay across the back as he had done a little while before. But there was one difference: in the cool shadow of the shelter the pony had been tied up, confined; here it was again a free agent, and the boy's heart raced before the decisive moment of swinging his leg over to the far side and sitting upright. At last he took a firm handful of mane and in one lithe movement straddled the pony for the second time. The white head swung up and for one terrifying moment the boy felt the bunching of great muscles in the back beneath him: felt the spine suddenly arch, the fore-legs jerk and the hindlegs crouch ready for the twisting leap and flight; saw the ears flatten against the straining neck and the eyes staring wildly, all this in the one moment before the colt again relaxed.

Philip sat holding his breath, but all was well, and the colt returned to its grazing. It was a little while before the boy ceased to tremble; the flash of insight into the physical strength of the animal beneath him had been disturbing. He sat quietly

102

for a little while getting used to the feeling of the live creature between his legs. The colt grazed on, apparently unaware of the boy on its back. He began to grow more confident; he felt relaxed and at home and now wanted to go farther. Gently but firmly he pulled the colt's head up with the halter rope; twice it tried to lower it again to graze but the boy insisted and finally it stood placidly.

How to make it move forward? The boy remembered the farmers on their ponies: Jerking once on the halter rope, he experimentally kicked the colt's ribs with both his heels at once. The sky spun, he had a fragmentary vision of a horizon that fell vertically from the sky to the ground and then the grass rose smoothly to meet him. He landed with a jarring shock, one arm underneath him, and lay there wondering calmly what it was all about. A sound caught his attention. He looked up and saw the white colt bucking, kicking, galloping in a frenzy; each time it bucked it squealed like a pig; the flying halter rope was flicking at its legs and sides, goading it to further fits of demented bucking. The boy closed his eyes and lay still, waiting. The colt ran until the fear died, then slowed down and finally stood at the far side of the field, its sides heaving, sweat making dark tracks down its legs. Painfully Philip rose to his feet. He was dizzy and his arm hurt but he was all right. He felt in his pocket for a bread crust and walked towards the distant pony. It regarded him with suspicion as he approached; once or twice it shied away, but he moved slowly and spoke gently and at last came within touching distance of it. He held the crust out towards the colt. It stretched its head timidly and accepted the bread. While it was chewing, the boy took a quiet step forward and got hold of the halter rope. The pony showed no further signs of distress and when Philip led off towards the gate it followed meekly, its flanks still heaving slightly. At the gate Philip gave it another piece of bread, stroked its neck one last time, then slipped the halter off and let it go. He leaned over the gate and watched it move away, grazing as it went. It appeared to be quite unaffected by the morning's events; not so the boy. As he watched the colt over the top of the gate he was no longer seeing the friendly companion of sun-drenched days on the moor; he was looking at an alien creature, loved yet feared.

The moorman had looked out of the window to see the colt careering around the paddock; at first it did not strike him as unusual until he noticed that it had its halter on. By the time he had got out into his garden the colt was standing quiet and Philip was getting to his feet. He was obviously not badly hurt and the old man relaxed. He could guess at what had occurred and was burning with curiosity to see what the boy would do. When he finally slipped the halter over the colt's head and let it go the old man returned to the house, still unseen.

Now he sat pensively in his worn armchair and wondered: What will he do now? As he thought about it a warm feeling of anticipation spread into his thoughts. What can he do? he thought. Where can he go for help? He wants to ride the pony. Who will help him? Suddenly things looked easier and he smiled. "He'll have to come to me," he said out loud and started to fill his pipe.

The morning after Philip's fall from the colt it started to rain and continued to do so for two days. During this time the boy did no more than make sure that the colt was still in the paddock. The rest of the time he spent in his room holding the halter and gazing out of the window over the rain-dimmed · moors, living over and over the morning that had seen so auspicious a beginning and so abrupt an end to the breaking-in of the colt. As he thought over every move he came to realise his mistake — the sudden puncturing of the gentle process by his thumping heels — but even with this knowledge the fear remained. It was not so much the fall through the air and the jarring crash as the terrifying revelation of potential violence in the bunching muscles and the enormous leap of the colt. Its whole presence in the boy's life had been one of companionship and gentleness; now he felt intuitively that the colt could kill him if it wished; he trembled and bit his lip as this fear flowed within him across and beneath the warm current of his love for the animal.

The morning of the third day dawned clear.

After breakfast the boy took the halter and some crusts of bread and went down to the paddock with his heart beating faster. For some time he led the pony about, stroking it and talking to it; then he led it to the shelter and tied it up as he had done three days before. Again he pulled up the bale of straw and stood on it, stroking and pressing down on the white back. Again he leaned over it until all his weight was lying across the colt's withers . . . but that was as far as he could go. The fear welled up in him and spread through his limbs; he lay there fighting to move, just to swing his leg over and sit up, but he could not. At last he slid back until his feet touched the ground and slumped to a sitting position on the bale. He put his head in his hands and waited for the trembling to stop. Once the colt turned to look at him, its thick white lashes throwing soft shadows across the blue of its eyes.

When the fear finally sank below the surface of his skin he got up and untied the colt, releasing it. He walked slowly across the field and out of the gate, not knowing what to do. As he turned towards home he looked once towards the low grey shape of the moorman's cottage and his heart ached.

Three times in two days the boy tried to mount the pony in the shelter at the far side of the paddock. Three times the paralysis of fear gripped his limbs and froze him where he lay uncomfortably across the withers. Three times he walked home again in growing despair. And each time the moorman watched from his garden, unseen by the boy. After the third time he decided to act.

106

Progress with Lady was slow. The old man could now feed her on the fist and hood her successfully, but only in the semidarkness of the shuttered mews. In her struggles on Philip's fist that fateful day she had broken two of the primarics on hcr lcft wing: two long pointed flight feathers without which her flying skill would be drastically reduced. These had to be repaired, and an assistant was needed for the rather delicate operation.

The moorman did not go to the boy's house; he telephoned and explained the idea to Mrs. Ransome. She agreed to ask Philip if he would help, without specifying what it was that was needed. A little later she rang back to say that the boy would be along that afternoon after tea. The old man prepared the necessary equipment and waited.

A little after five o'clock there was a faint tap at the door; the moorman opened it and took the boy into his study. When he had closed the door he said to the boy: "Now, Philip, if you'll wait here for a moment, I'll fetch Lady and explain what I want you to do."

At the mention of the hawk the boy looked up quickly and then down again, but not before the old man had seen the pain there. He went out to the garden to fetch Lady, praying that the boy would not run away before he could return. He need not have worried; Philip was sitting where he had left him, his hands clasped together, his eyes lowered.

The moorman had hooded Lady; she was not ready for carriage yet, and anyway she would have to be hooded for the operation ahead. She sat absolutely still on his fist; as the boy looked at her his face twisted and his eyes brimmed suddenly with tears. The old man was moved, but forced himself to speak quietly and normally.

"Now lad, you see that silk handkerchief on the table beside you? Pick it up, will you, and spread it out in both hands."

The boy did so, tears running down his face.

"Good. Now I want you to do this very gently: wrap the handkerchief around her, from behind, and take hold of her carefully with both hands, keeping your thumbs pointing up towards her head. Do you see what I mean?"

The boy nodded and did as he was asked.

"Right, now hold on to her. Do you see the cushion on the table? I want you to lay her down onto it, face down, so that her head sticks out over the edge, but so that her body is on the cushion."

The boy laid her down gently and stood holding her. The moorman drew the yellow feet back by pulling slowly on the leash; he bent down and said to the boy: "Now, lift your foot," then slipped the leash underneath it. "Right, foot down and stay like that. All right?"

The boy nodded; the hawk remained quite still and relaxed. Through the silk handkerchief the boy could feel her heart beating steadily. The moorman spread the left wing and smoothed out the two broken feathers. Taking a scalpel, he carefully cut through the shaft of each, a little above the break, leaving the web perfect on either side of the cut. He then selected a feather from a little heap on the table and held it over the first of the two broken primaries, adjusting it until it extended as far as the original had done. Marking carefully with his thumb-nail the point at which it coincided with the cut in the primary beneath it, he took the scalpel and made another incision; this left him with a section of feather that was almost exactly the same as the part missing from the kestrel's wing. The old man glanced up at the boy: he was watching, absorbed. The old man said quietly:

"This is called 'imping' the broken primaries. It's a very old word — even Shakespeare used it. I'll find the quotation when we've finished."

The boy nodded, almost imperceptibly. Now the moorman went through the same process for the second primary, so that he had two trimmed sections ready. He then picked up an "imping needle," a piece of piano wire about an inch long, filed at each end to a point; smearing a strong glue on to one end he carefully inserted it into the hollow quill of the new section of feather; then, smearing glue on to the projecting half of the needle, he pushed it gently into the shaft of the broken feather. He repeated the operation on the second feather and then stepped back to inspect the job. The joins were scarcely visible: even the dark bars on the new sections were the same as on Lady's wing; they were, in fact, taken from her own feathers, lost during a moult and carefully saved by Barry for just such a contingency as this.

Satisfied, the moorman glanced at Philip. The boy looked up, his eyes shining, and smiled quickly; then looked down again at the motionless hawk, its wings folded again. The old man knew then that it had not been in vain: that far more had been repaired than two broken feathers. Carefully he took the little hawk from the boy's hands.

"Thank you, lad — I couldn't have managed it without you. Now sit down while I put her away and we'll have a cup of tea."

Later, over tea, he ferreted for and found the quotation he had mentioned; he read it out to the boy:

> " 'If, then, we shall shake off our slavish yoke,
> Imp out our drooping country's broken wing.'

Do you see what he means by that?"

The boy thought for a moment, then looked up and nodded.

"I th-think so. Y-y-yes, I do."

The moorman closed the book and laid it down on the table. The boy spoke:

"D-do you know any m-m-more?"

"Only one, and I can't remember all of that. Sir Toby Belch calls somebody a "coward and a coystril" because he won't drink a toast to his niece."

The boy smiled faintly.

"Th-that's not very n-nice, is it?"

The moorman shook his head.

"There's an even worse one I found in Roget: 'the swarming rabble of our coistrell curates.' I'm afraid that in those days the word was used for a knave, a bad number."

110

The old man leaned forward and poured him-self another cup of tea. Without looking at the boy he said: "Philip, if you need any help with your pony, just let me know."

The boy did not reply; looked down into his teacup with a slight frown on his forehead. Care-fully now, the moorman thought, carefully.

"It's a help sometimes. In fact, it's almost im-possible to train any animal without a certain amount of help. You do want to ride your pony, don't you?" The boy nodded. Stirring his tea, the moorman said: "Then you'll need a hand. You've helped me with my problem; I'll help you with yours. Shall we make a start tomorrow?"

Philip nodded again. Thank God, the moor-man thought. Now it'll be all right.

It was not until he was in bed that night that the moorman remembered his promise to Barry: that if the colt were to be found he would send Lady back to him. He lay there aghast at the realisation. Even after he had rationalised the whole situation — that he could not have sent back a ruined hawk; that he would reclaim her and then send her back — he could not throw off the feeling of guilt. He decided to write to his friend the next day and tell him the whole story; but even after this decision he lay awake for hours and when he slept at last his sleep was troubled.

The next morning they started on the pony. The boy had been surprisingly orthodox in his attempt at backing the colt, up to where he had used his heels. The moorman now took him through the same stages, and when the boy was at last sitting upright on the pony's back, his face white with tension, the old man led the colt quietly around the field until the boy relaxed. At the end of the first session when they slipped the halter over the colt's head and allowed it to wander away the boy's eyes were shining. All his old confidence in the moorman had come flooding back and as they walked back to the cottage he positively chattered in his exuberance.

That evening Mrs. Ransome telephoned. She appeared to be as excited as the boy had been: Philip was more than restored, he was radiant. When the old man had put the receiver down he walked over to the dresser and poured himself a liberal portion of Johnny Walker. As he sat back in his armchair, sipping reflectively, he thought: I wish hawks were reclaimed as quickly as people. He knew that the sentiment was inaccurate, to say the least, but it fitted the situation well enough so he let it stand.

A few days later, a reply came from Barry.

"Dear Colonel,

"Thank you for your letter.

"I am most relieved to hear that Lady is coming on well after her little episode.

"When I first read your letter I found myself wishing that you had written to tell me of her condition straight away, but after thinking about it for a while I decided that you behaved quite reasonably in leaving it; I would only have worried unnecessarily, and anyway she could not be in better hands than your own."

God bless you, the old man thought, but you could easily be wrong. Easily.

"As you have gone so far with reclaiming her, I think it best that she stay with you until she is back to normal, as you suggest. But please, please will you let me know as soon as you think she is all right and I shall come down and fetch her.

"Don't worry about what has happened (I know you will, but don't), it wasn't your fault, and I still think that it was a good idea for Philip to have her. Incidentally, if you think it would be all right, I would like to meet him when I come down for Lady; please, when you write, tell me how he is getting on — the boy I mean.

"So glad you found the pony.

"Looking forward to hearing from you.

Barry."

The colt was coming along well. As soon as it was thoroughly backed and would allow Philip to vault on and off without flinching, the moorman introduced both it and the boy to the art of lungeing.

He had got the idea of a sustained early training on the lunge from an old friend, a contemporary of his schooldays named Roy Kelting. Some years before, the moorman had watched

113

Roy lungeing a child and had noticed immediately the child's beautiful seat and balance and the pony's obedient manner. Now, years later, he remembered that day and decided to put the theory into practice.

After a couple of days the colt was walking and trotting quietly around the old man at the end of the lungeing-rein. As the days went by he showed the boy how the pony learned its aids first from the voice, going forward obediently at the order "Walk on!," into a relaxed trot at the order "Ter-rot!," and down again to a walk at the order "and wa-a-alk"; then a halt and perhaps a handful of grass before going on to the other rein and a repetition of the lesson.

The moorman raised the question of bitting. Had Philip a bridle, or would he like to borrow one? The boy, remembering his antipathy towards the bit, demurred; but the old man explained that they could not do a proper job without one, and anyway a snaffle bit was only severe if it were misused. At last the boy gave in and fetched the old bridle that he had hidden away in his wardrobe; but about a saddle he was adamant: He did not want a saddle; he would not have a saddle; and on this point the moorman gave way. He'll probably find it so uncomfortable when he gets going, he thought, that he'll beg for one.

So they progressed: The colt working on the lunge, chewing the unfamiliar bit; the boy sitting bareback, learning to relax and allow his body to go with the pony's movements; holding the mane for support, then letting go for brief periods so as

114

to improve his balance. The old man was an experienced instructor. He had learned to ride the hard way, at Weedon, as a young man. Later he had returned there as an instructor. His methods were not modern, but they were admirably suited to the job in hand. Philip was spending as much as an hour a day on the lunge, spread over two or three sessions.

As the colt trotted steadily around he would release the mane and raise his arms to shoulder-level. Then, to the moorman's orders, he would swing them from side to side, up and down, together and alternately; touch his toes, one at a time and both together; lie back until his head touched the pony's rump; then he would pick up the reins, knotted over the colt's withers, and take a gentle contact, learning how to keep his wrists supple so that his hands could move with the colt's head and keep a "living" contact on the bit. Between sessions on the lunge the old man would lead the pony about the paddock and out on to the road, the boy still keeping the lightest of contacts on the bit.

One day the old man decided to take a step forward.

"Now hold on to the mane, Philip. I'm going to ask him to canter. You'll find the movement very different from the trot, but so long as you relax your body, keep your legs still and hold on to the mane, you'll be all right."

He called out in clear, ringing tones: "And can-ter!" at the same time swinging the long whip towards the colt's quarters. It went into a fast raking trot, the boy holding on as his head went

115

up and down, his body shaken by the jarring pace. Again: "Can-ter!" and again the whip curling towards the quarters. At last the pony broke into a canter. Immediately the motion changed from the jarring discomfort of the fast trot to the wonderful, indescribable surge and pause of the canter. To the boy it felt like waves rolling into the shore, one after the other; great massive, surging waves, and he riding them, lordly and relaxed. All too soon the moorman brought the pony down through trot and walk to a halt, where it stood obediently, its sides heaving a little as the old man made in to it and gave it a handful of grass as a reward. The boy's eyes were shining as he patted the colt's neck.

"C-can we d-do that every d-d-day?"

The old man chuckled. "Nearly every day, lad. Must give him the odd rest, you know."

And all the time the moorman worked steadily and patiently to restore the little hawk to sanity. After many setbacks she began to make ground and was soon going over her original training with an air of casual intimacy. Only occasionally something would happen and she would seem to go berserk: bating with a sustained fury that left her panting and weak and the old man plunged in despair. However, these fits became fewer and further between, and he began to look forward to the day when he would be able to reunite her with the boy. He fully intended returning her to Barry as soon as she was ready — almost as soon, that is. The idea had grown in his mind that it would help the boy to have her for a few days and see that she had fully recovered from the damage he had caused before she finally returned to her owner.

CHAPTER VII

AUGUST SLIPPED UNNOTICED into September. The weather, uncertain all the summer, seemed to mellow, become rich and mature; the golden autumn sunshine held a promise that the summer had withheld. "Hurting" began, the ancient annual harvesting of the bilberry, or whortleberry. Children, old people, and the otherwise unoccupied went out in the morning and returned with baskets brimming with the waxlike fruit, the children with carmine stains around their mouths and all with purple fingers. While men harvested the bilberries, birds fed on the berries of the rowan; blackberries appeared in their glistening clusters on banks and woodsides. The moors began to flame, to turn russet and brown, and all the while the sun shone kindly and clouds were high.

Towards the end of the second week in September the moorman received a letter from Barry.

"Dear Colonel,

"Thank you for your letter. I am glad to hear that Lady is almost back to normal — will you ring me as soon as she is ready so that I can collect her?

"I am rather worried about my Gos — she was in great yarak but I know that something is wrong with her although I cannot pin it down. Let's hope it is just a passing upset. It is rather a shame because the weather is so perfect, but I dare not fly her until I know what is wrong with her.

"Hope you are well — looking forward to receiving a clearance for Lady!

Yours ever,
Barry."

In spite of the light tone of the letter, the moorman thought that he detected a note of worry. He wrote back, the same day.

"Dear Barry,

"Yes, Lady is almost back in shape again. In fact, you could come for her any time (or I could bring her up to you) but I have one last boon to ask of you: May I please keep her just long enough to effect a reintroduction to the boy? This will be so good for him that I am emboldened to ask you.

"If, for any reason at all, you would rather have her back straight away, then let me know and we can arrange it immediately, but I do hope you will agree to just another week or so.

"Sorry to hear about your Gos — I hope it

119

is all cleared up now and that you are able to benefit from our 'Indian Summer.'

My regards to your family,
Jonathan Lane-Forster."

Two mornings later an overnight telegram arrived: "Agreed. Barry." The moorman began to arrange the reunion.

By this time both the boy and the colt had got as far as coming off the lunge and going for short rides together. The boy was a natural horseman and the old man's meticulous training had made a fairly competent rider of him. He still had a lot to learn, of course, but he was going in the right direction; as a result of those long hours on the lunge he had a marvellously easy, deceptively strong seat, and the pony was going kindly for him.

Philip's first ride out on to the moor had been one of the happiest experiences of his life. The feeling of freedom and of the living animal between his legs had gone to his head and he had laughed and sung like a fool while the white colt had walked steadily and sedately, reaching down occasionally to snatch at a frond of bracken.

At home, too, things were developing. Mrs. Ransome, following the moorman's lead, was no longer watching the boy's every movement. She had learned how to go about her business and appear to ignore him. When their eyes met now she would smile quickly and look away again; as often as not he would smile back at her and continue watching her as she moved away. The boy was growing towards her now, and her eyes had lost their hopeless hunger.

As days went by, everything was developing and improving: the boy, the colt, and the hawk. The moorman watched his three plots beginning to fructify after his intensive cultivation and was content.

At last he decided to take the plunge and try to reunite the hawk and the boy. They had never mentioned the events of that terrible day, either of them, and the old man found it difficult to broach the subject. He decided finally not to announce it, but to simply bring it about. One afternoon he took the boy back with him and led him to the mews; having first lowered the blind, thus darkening the interior, he entered and motioned Philip to join him, then closed the door behind them.

When the boy's eyes had adjusted to the darkness, he was just able to pick out the shape of the little falcon; he could see the dark, shining beak and the brilliant eye as she turned her head this way and that, trying to identify her visitors. Saying nothing, the moorman took down his gauntlet from its nail and handed it to Philip. As he pulled it on, the boy's heart was pounding so that he was not sure that he could not actually hear it, but the old man seemed not to notice. Philip moved nearer to the screen perch as the moorman tugged at his sleeve; he heard rather than saw the old man untying the leash, and then felt it being wrapped around his little finger. He heard the moorman whisper "Go ahead," and with his breathing tight in his throat he pressed gently on Lady's hind claws. She stepped back and up on to his fist, exactly as she had on their first meeting. He felt the moorman touch his right arm; looking round he saw a hand holding something and took it: it was a piece of kidney. He took the hint and presented the titbit to the falcon; she took it eagerly, and he felt her talons clench a little in excitement. Again he fed her, and again. Now the moorman tugged at his sleeve a second time and they moved towards the door. As it opened slowly and the evening sun streamed in, Philip saw her gazing eagerly towards the light, anticipating exercise. The door was fully open now and still she sat relaxed, even rousing her feathers once. They moved slowly out of the mews, the moorman standing close on Philip's right so that the hawk could see him. The boy could see his arm trembling with the tension, but Lady still seemed to notice nothing amiss and was looking chirpily around for diversions. The moorman let out a long, long breath and relaxed.

"Well, lad, everything seems to be in order."

Philip smiled wanly and began to speak: "D-d-did you —"

Then Lady bated.

With fury, with terror, with what seemed to be the intention of self-destruction she flew fast and hard down, down, down, towards the earth, straining at the jesses until the boy thought that they must break. They stood, absolutely helpless, waiting for the storm to abate.

At last it did. Philip put his right hand under the hawk's breast and lifted her lightly on to the fist again. She sat gaping, panting with exhaustion, her eyes crazy.

Suddenly the moorman saw that there was still a chance. Exultantly he reached into his pocket for another piece of kidney, handed it to the boy and said:

"Put it in her mouth, lad, quickly!"

Philip took it and in one movement pushed it right into the hawk's open beak. Lady shook her head violently and the piece of meat flew sideways to the ground.

"Again," said the moorman, "quickly!"

Again the scrap of kidney shot out of her beak as she refused.

"Again."

And this time . . . this time . . . as if nothing was wrong, Lady swallowed the meat. She seemed to relax, to straighten somehow; her eyes were wide but not crazy, her beak was almost closed, and when Philip offered her the next piece of kidney she took it eagerly.

It had all happened so quickly that they had hardly been able to comprehend events; but now, with the battle behind them, both the old man and the boy felt suddenly weak at the knees. The moorman laughed briefly and rubbed his face with his hand.

"Thank God," he said simply, then grew serious once more.

"Philip, try saying something again."

The boy tried:

"B-b-b-but wh-wh-what?" hardly able to get a word out in the stress of his emotion. The moorman smiled.

"That will do very well," he said, and the boy smiled back at him brilliantly. The little falcon finished the kidney, shuffled her feet, stretched first one wing and then the other, roused her feathers and then sat for a moment or two in complete contentment.

It was then that she crowned the whole episode with pure farce: loudly and unmistakably she burped.

The old man stepped quickly behind the wall of the shed and doubled up with silent laughter that had in it a ring of mild hysteria. He had to move out of sight or his actions might have frightened the now cheerful little hawk. Fortunately for them both Philip was too surprised to be affected in the same way.

The old man recovered at last, and emerged from behind the mews.

"All right, lad, you pass. Now put her away and come into the house; we'll have a cup of tea."

Philip was becoming quite fond of tea.

Then began the halcyon days for Philip, with his white colt and his hawk. The fine spell continued, stretching languidly into late September. From nine o'clock in the morning until after sunset, until that time once known in the old Dartmoor dialect as "dimpsy," the boy was out on the moors with one or the other of his loves. After supper he would sit in the living room with his parents, reading or drawing quietly. Though still unable to talk to his mother, a language of looks was growing between them. So infectious was the boy's happiness and growing confidence that they permeated the whole house; his mother moved lightly and sang over the dishes and at the ironing board; even his father would speak to him occasionally, then laugh in embarrassment and return to his newspaper or book.

Philip was riding now far and wide; the understanding between the boy and the pony was an unusually complete thing; boy and animal seemed to merge at times, their movements so entangled that it seemed that the colt's strong heart was driving the boy's blood through his veins, the boy's brain flexing and extending the colt's perfect limbs.

Together they explored the wild and beautiful places within their reach: Wistman's Wood, Tavy Cleave, Dartmeet (full of trippers — on quickly to the wild height of Yar Tor). Resting sometimes, the boy would fall asleep; the pony would graze nearby, its halter rope dragging. When the boy woke he would stand up and call "Philip!" and the colt would trot back to him, whickering through its soft nostrils and blowing heather-scented breath at his face in intimate recognition. The boy could not understand now why he had named the colt with his own name, but could find no alternative so it stuck.

Out with Lady the boy would thrill to her sharp-winged cleanness, her sleek streamlined slicing of the still air to alight on his raised fist, fluttering like a soft brown-barred moth; watching her soar and winnow, riding the thermals; spiralling lazily on dragonfly wings; stooping in vertical hunger to the lure and mantling luxuriously over it, her gleaming gun-metal and grey wing-feathers shooting showers of sun sparks on to the ochre moor grass.

On September 28th, clouds began to gather on the eastern edge of the moor and a cool breeze played gently with the fronds of bracken. The moorman received a letter marked "Express" from Barry.

"Dear Colonel,

"Thank you for your letter and for your encouraging news about Lady.

"My Gos died three days ago. I got the vet to do a post-mortem and it turned out to be Aspergillosis. He showed me her lungs — they were almost completely destroyed. God only knows how she stayed alive as long as she did.

"You can guess, I am sure, what all this is leading up to: I've really got to have Lady back. You told me that her reunion with Philip was a success, so may I assume that she has done her job?

"It is rather lonely about the place with no hungry beaks to gape at me. I always kept at least two hawks for that reason — they are so fragile, poor things.

"Please telephone me as soon as you get this letter so that we can arrange Lady's return. I will come down for her myself — I would like a change.

"I am sure you will realise that this time I really do need her back.

Looking forward to hearing from you,
Barry."

The moorman telephoned immediately. Barry wanted to drive down the following day but the old man persuaded him to postpone his journey by one day, so as to give Philip a chance to get used to the idea. After a slight hesitation, Barry agreed.

That afternoon, when Philip took Lady out on to the moor, the old man went with him. Over by the old tin-workings where the larks were ringing up in their dozens he told the boy about the death of Barry's goshawk and his consequent duty to send Lady back to him. Philip knew the sensation of losing a well-loved animal and he saw immediately that it was the only thing to do. As he watched the kestrel winnowing above in the strengthening breeze he said: "Anyway, it w-w-wouldn't be fair f-for m-me to have b-b-both when he hasn't g-got anything."

The next morning the boy came to the moorman with a request; he had often thought about taking out Lady with the colt together, rather than separately, and on this last day with the little hawk he wanted to try it. He had seen, in the moorman's books on falconry, old prints of horsemen with falcons on the fist, and ever since he had dreamed of riding his colt at a sedate canter across the moor with Lady, like a royal peregrine, swaying and gripping on the gauntlet.

The old man did not entirely like the idea, but the boy looked so pleadingly at him that he agreed.

"But don't fly her unless you get off and do it from the ground; remember that Barry is coming for her tomorrow and we don't want her raking off on her own."

He held Lady while the boy bridled and mounted the colt. Handing her up and helping to arrange the leash around the boy's fingers, he frowned slightly.

"Do be careful, lad. It would be terrible if anything were to happen to her. Don't go too far, and go quietly; right?" The boy nodded.

As an afterthought the moorman said: "By the way, where are you going to take her? I'd better know, in case."

"B-b-braky Firs," the boy replied immediately; it was one of his favourite haunts. The old man nodded and patted the colt gently on the rump.

"Off you go then. Don't stay out too long."

As the boy rode away, the kestrel perched happily on his fist, the moorman suddenly wanted to run after the boy, call out, tell him to come back, stop him somehow.

"Silly fool," he muttered to himself, "be sensible." But as he walked slowly back to the house he knew that he was gambling with something that was not his.

High clouds like tattered grey blankets were streaming across the sky in unending procession; as they hid the sun the air cooled. A breeze was blowing that smelt of the Atlantic and deserted shore lines. The white colt lifted its head and drank the wind, the horizon in its blue eyes. As the boy's body moved with the colt, he held his forearm steady and the little hawk roused her feathers in pleasure at the freshening breeze and looked about her brightly.

At the bottom of the hill leading towards Sherberton the boy turned off to the right and began to follow the Swincombe down towards Swincombe Meet, where it flowed into the West Dart; the peat-tinged water chuckled and rushed as it broke over rocks and swirled across shallows, gold-flecked in the moving sunlight. Along the flat ground that followed the river, Philip urged the colt quietly into a canter. As the pony went into its gait he leaned forward slightly, his whole body supple, swinging rhythmically with the movement. At the first acceleration the little hawk had tensed, crouching suddenly, gripping his fist and opening her beak; now she rode with him, crouching still, her wings half-open, her tail fanned, looking suddenly fierce with her hooked beak thrust forward and her yellow talons braced and clenched. The colt's long mane boiled and whipped like the crest of a breaker as it went forward at a powerful controlled canter, keen on the bit, its nostrils flared and showing crimson centres, yet obedient and collected, flowing forward through the bracken like a high-masted ship. The boy felt like a god: The vital wind that scorched his lungs acted like wine and he was a little drunk with it, they were all three drunk with it, the pony as it devoured the rolling ground with its forward-flung white limbs, and the hawk too, who half-flew at the boy's side, her muscles like fine steel in the long earthbound stoop towards Braky Firs.

As they approached the rougher ground, the boy pulled up and continued at a walk, he and the pony breathing deeply, the kestrel still tense, her wings slightly unfolded and hunched, as though about to take off. Suddenly a shot rang out over the hill, followed by a clamour of rooks. The colt shied violently, Philip felt himself falling, saw the ground hurtling up towards him, had a sudden terrible vision of Lady crushed beneath him and with a convulsive effort threw her violently away from him a split second before he hit the ground.

He rolled and was back on his feet in one movement, his eyes sweeping the sky. She was climbing fast into the wind, the leash trailing behind her like the tail of a comet. Over the pine trees that clothed the hill he saw rooks swirling upwards, thrown into panic by the shot. Lady veered sharply, swung round on momentarily still wings, her tail spread wide, then joined her strength to the wind's own terrible power and hurtled down the sky, her leash jerking and leaping after her like a lunatic's terror.

The boy's heart turned to ice: Wide-eyed and silent in the extremity of his fear he jumped at the trembling pony, swung on to its back and closed his legs sharply. As the colt leaped forward the boy tangled his fingers in the mane for purchase and screamed at it. His eyes followed the hawk as she dropped down the sky towards the far side of the hill and he rode like a maniac across its broken slope. Just before Lady disappeared below the crown of the hill another shot rang out, clear and flat. He saw her jerk once, as though flicked by an invisible finger, and then she dropped out of sight. A cry was torn up out of his throat and he kicked and flailed at the colt's sides as it ran like blown spray across the treacherous surface and over the brow of the hill, its ears flat back, its eyes staring, its mane and tail like a waterfall, streaming down the bitter wind.

He soon found her. She was a little tumbled heap of feathers in the moor-grass. Like a broken moth she lay, her perfect wings half-closed, her bright eyes dulled already by the breath of dying. The cream-sienna of her breast feathers was broken by two scarlet stains that glistened in the weak sunlight. Here and there little downy feathers blew and caught in the heather, tumbled and drifted as though trying to escape, to leave behind the place of death.

Philip slid off the pony's back and stood looking down at the pathetic little thing. Suddenly he clenched his fists and swung round to face the dark pine woods where death was lurking.

"Where are you?" he screamed. "Who are you?"

His voice sounded small in all that moving air. There was no reply from the trees; he never saw the face of death. There was only a silence that was not wide enough to cover nor deep enough to drown death's guilt as it crouched somewhere waiting for the boy to go away.

Philip turned back to Lady. He took off the useless gauntlet and dropped it; then he sank to his knees and tenderly gathered up the broken creature. He closed her wings, laid her in his lap and stroked her feathers smooth. A tear fell from his cheek on to her back; it ran quickly over the soft feathers and mixed at once with the blood that had already ceased to flow. All the time the colt stood nearby, its head hanging, its sides heaving, one hind leg resting; sweat and blood from thorn scratches mixed to paint thin pink lines down its limbs, and it was trembling slightly in the cold wind. Its blue eyes were dull beneath half-lowered lashes.

Not knowing quite what he did, Philip gently removed the leash and then the jesses from the dead falcon's legs. Then he stood up and, opening the buttons down the front of his shirt, laid her inside, against the warmth of his skin. He led the apathetic pony to a rock and mounted it slowly, one hand protectively over the shape inside his shirt.

In the trodden grass lay the leash, trailing and discarded, the swivel gleaming dully as the sun came out and then disappeared again; the jesses lay nearby, unfamiliar on their own, there on the dying grass; they were curled into a half-circle as though trying to get back to their long-worn shape; the forgotten gauntlet lying on its back.

The moorman had worried without cease after Philip's departure. Less than an hour later he was walking to meet them, trying to rationalise his anxiety. He saw the distant speck and put up his field glasses expectantly. A stillness descended over the old man as he lowered the glasses, and he shivered. He stood motionless as the boy approached, the pony walking wearily, stumbling from time to time as it climbed the long hill towards the waiting figure.

As the boy drew up to him the old man suddenly saw the open shirt and a dark stain at the boy's waist. He started forward, alarmed.

"Are you all right, lad?"

Then he stopped and understood as the boy reached in and took out the limp body, still warm from nestling against his side. He handed the broken thing to the old man and then sent the pony on again wearily, sitting slumped, one hand hanging down at his side. The moorman did not look after him. He stood gazing down at the body of Lady as it rested in his gnarled hands, the beautiful head lolling back, the beak slightly open.

A little later he telephoned Barry. His friend came to the telephone brimming with good spirits. He listened in silence as the old man told him haltingly what had happened. When he had finished there was no sound at the other end of the line.

"Are you there, Barry?" said the old man.

"Yes, I'm here," Barry said and rang off.

The moorman sat for a few seconds with the dialling tone buzzing in his ear, then gently re-

133

placed the receiver and sat staring straight ahead. This was the most terrible part of it all: that he had asked, asked, asked; and Barry had given, given, given: and just at the point where it could all have been reversed and sent flowing the other way, it had been stopped, dead. Now and forever the old man had taken everything and had given nothing in return, no matter what he might do in the future. The enormous double injustice of it blinded the old man's eyes and for the second time in two months he felt himself adrift on a still sea of despair.

CHAPTER VIII

P HILIP DID NOT SUFFER the setback from
Lady's death that the moorman thought he might.
He grieved, certainly, but appeared almost more
concerned over the colt, who proved to be slightly
lame the next day. It was the moorman who
suffered this time. When Philip had temporarily
ruined the hawk, the day he had seen the colt on
the moor, the old man had experienced anger,
frustration, guilt, and impatience, all emotions
and soon forgotten; it was the boy who had been
wounded that day. Now the old man felt the bolt
of grief biting deep into him, shattering the serenity that had settled over him in later years. He
knew that the matter could not be allowed to rest
on the strength of one brief telephone call, so he
decided to write.

"Dear Barry,
    "I don't have to describe to you my feelings
after the loss of your hawk.

"Even though the incident itself was purely accidental, and as such, beyond my control, the final responsibility rests with me.

"I wish that I could communicate to you my knowledge of the fact, gathered after many trials, that life puts everything right in its own way — that the deepest grief becomes first bearable and at last unimportant — but I'm afraid I cannot. You will have to learn for yourself, as did I.

"I do not expect you to reply to this letter nor do I expect to hear from you for quite some time. I only ask that, when that time comes when you can regard this whole episode with equanimity, you get in touch with me.

"I value your friendship and do not wish to lose it entirely.

Yours ever,
Jonathan Lane-Forster."

In spite of saying that he expected no reply from Barry, he nourished a secret hope that there would, in fact, be one; but the days passed and none came; finally he lost hope and settled down to wait. And all the while he covered his secret pain and wore an exterior normality when with Philip; the business of Lady had to be forgotten and forgotten quickly, or it might retard the boy's progress.

There had been a brief agonising scene when the distraught boy arrived at his home that evening and tried to apologise for what he had done. The old man was shocked by the boy's evident distress: He appeared to be on the verge of a nervous breakdown. He walked back to the boy's home with him, rationalising, reassuring, trying to reduce the whole thing to a minor accident.

So it was that when Philip called at his cottage the next morning with the news that the pony was lame, the old man assumed a cheerful air and went with him to the field to see for himself. It was not serious, obviously, but the colt was definitely lame in its near-fore. The moorman felt a slight puffiness just below the fetlock and decided to call in the vet.

Hugh Otterburn was a young man, not long in practice. He came out immediately and looked the colt over.

"It's only a mild strain," he said straightening up. "Rest him for a week, then take him quietly for a few days. He should be right as rain."

The boy nodded.

"And those feet want trimming, too," Hugh said, pointing at the slight cracks forming at the tip of the hoof. Philip looked questioningly at the moorman.

"I'll see to that, my boy," he said, "don't worry."

When the boy had taken the halter off the pony and left for home, the moorman took Hugh's arm and started to move him towards the cottage.

"Come along in, Hugh, you've got time for a drink, haven't you?"

"Thank you, sir. I'm off duty now, so I will. No need to worry about breathing gin at anxious poodles."

They passed from the cold, rather sad morning into the homely comfort of the old man's study.

While the white pony was resting its strained tendon it was bought by the moorman. He had made a long sketch of the brand and had sent it to a friend who was a member of the Breed Society with a note asking him if he would trace the registered owner. The reply came on October 2nd, and contained the name and address of a landowner near Moretonhampstead. The moorman rang him and arranged to visit him. He sat over a mug of homemade cider at the plain wood table in the long low-ceilinged kitchen and told the story of Philip and the colt. The landowner, countryman through and through, was less interested in the story once he had grasped that the moorman wanted to buy the colt. Before the old man had finished the story he dismissed it with a wave of his hand and got down to business. In a surprisingly short time the colt had changed hands for forty-five guineas. The moorman wrote a cheque and left; the whole business had taken less than half an hour. That evening he telephoned Philip's mother and told her about the transaction. Philip did not even know that he had suddenly, in the eyes of the law, acquired a pony.

The long weeks of patient training with the pony and the hawk had left the old man little time for anything else. Now, with the colt resting and Philip quite content to stay at home when not seeing to its needs, he started again to take long walks over the moor, on his own. With his old stick he travelled miles over the grey solitudes, breathing in the pure rain-washed air, seeking again his previous serenity. The moors, so silent yet so turbulent with the singing of running water, began to heal his wound.

October had brought with it the final death of the late summer. Soft misty rains fell, swelling the streams until they boiled white between their banks. Following the Dart down from Hexworthy, past the old tin-workings, the moorman clambered over the piled boulders beneath the stunted oaks that lined the steep banks. Mosses and maidenhair ferns hung from the low branches; lichens threw vivid spreading blots of rust and ochre across trees and rocks alike; pale convoluted fungi rose from beneath the litter of dead leaves and projected startlingly from the glistening trunks. Past this dell, the moorman strode across the meadows that led him to Dartmeet. Standing on the hump-backed bridge, staring down mesmerised at the boiling flood beneath, the words of the old Dartmoor chant came into his mind:

"Dart, Dart, wants a heart . . ."

Suddenly the river was malignant, crowding and spitting up at him, snarling deep in its murky bowels, thundering against the stone piles of the bridge until they trembled. Anger flowered ridiculously in the old man's half hypnotised brain. You've had your heart, damn you, he thought bitterly. Then he walked away, feeling the rage subside within him, leaving him weak.

The moorman quickly realised that the colt's

lameness was helping to keep the boy's thoughts from dwelling on his terrible experience with Lady. To further the process he suggested that Philip should hosepipe the colt's leg three times a day, as though it were an afterthought of the vet's. It did no harm and kept the boy far more occupied than before. Nine days after the accident Philip rode the colt for a short way at a quiet walk; it appeared sound to the watching moorman, and a few days after that he gave the go-ahead to ride it normally again.

The boy had changed since the colt's blue eyes had first challenged and held his own, that grey March day. He was more assured, more definite, less absorbed in his private world than before. He was still painfully shy before strangers, but he was giving more trust to his parents as well as to the moorman. Before his movements had been clumsy and self-conscious; now he moved with a certain gravity and care. He was beginning to participate in the daily routine of home-life, more than ever before. His mother would remember those terrible long drawn-out battles of will against will and wonder how she could have been so blind. She felt a new woman; the fierceness and the militancy had gone out of her love; she was slower and calmer now, and cared less about trifles. Not only the boy but also her husband felt this change in her and there was an imperceptible drawing in of the family unit, each towards the other. The moorman felt something of this when he went into the house, and knew that — whatever the cost — his work and care had not been in vain. Philip was withdrawing steadily from his other world and was learning to take a place in the society of human beings. Although he had become very fond of the boy, the old man now felt that it was time to fade gradually away into the background. In spite of the improvement in Philip's relations with his parents, it was still to the moorman that he turned for help or for comfort, and to the moorman that he now spoke most. The old man knew that if he could effect a gradual retreat, it would encourage Philip to turn to his parents; once this happened, the old man felt intuitively, the way would be clear for the boy to break down the final barrier and begin to talk to them. Philip's improvement towards normality had about it a feeling of progress and inevitability; the old man, having done so much to set it in motion, did not now wish to impede it. It was a hard decision to make, but once made he found it easier than he had anticipated to maintain; something independent and irascible in the old man's nature had always caused him to shun situations where he might become the recipient of too much affection. For this reason he had never kept a dog, but always a cat.

So he started to roam the moors again and when at home invented little jobs that left Philip much more to his own devices than before. He continued to show an interest in the colt and he and Philip would spend hours together in his study when the weather was bad, looking at books about horsemanship and stable management.

There followed a time of grey blustering days

on the moor with frequent squalls and fleeting patches of watery sunshine. Browns predominated everywhere, broken only by the grey of the granite and the startling green of the sphagnum in the ubiquitous bogs.

The boy rode far and free. His relationship with the colt also had developed. There had been a kind of equality between them in the early days, the boy even going a little in awe of the wild blue eyes; but now he was master, and the colt served him. Served him well too: going with an *élan* that seemed an echo of the great sweeping winds that blew high over the moor. The boy had not ceased to love the animal — far from it: his affection for it was charged with tenderness and concern. But he was the master; and the colt knew it and seemed to strive to please him. When the wind picked them up in its boisterous arms and threw them ahead of it, the colt would gallop like Pegasus, hooves seeming hardly to touch the ground, long mane lashing Philip's face. At such times a horse's body takes on a quality that is almost terrifying: in place of the supple flex and swing that relaxes the rider's body, there is a sudden hardness, a rocklike obduracy: The legs pound like pistons, jarring, jolting; the flattened ears and the bulging eyes seem to belong to another creature; the muscles bunch and whip; the very coat seems to be of spun steel. Speed — so remote in a car or an aeroplane — is suddenly an intensely personal reality.

All this Philip learned and more, far more. He became exacting: demanded that the colt obey him without question; that it cease to snatch

142

at grass and heather as it went along; that it stand quietly if he so desired. Under the boy's loving yet firm tutelage and the moorman's distant supervision, the colt grew up, matured, became strong and graceful, responsive to every movement of the boy's body and every word. The boy also was maturing in just the same way.

The old man enjoyed his occasional evenings with Philip who was becoming good company — no longer the wide-eyed, pale, awkward figure of earlier days; a more relaxed and talkative person altogether. Even the stammer was slowly easing, giving the boy the confidence to embark upon longer sentences with complete equanimity.

November was a soft month; skies were uniformly grey and low, hanging fine curtains of rain across the middle distances. There was water everywhere: rushing boisterously red-brown in the rivers and streams, dripping perpetually from branches and fronds of bracken, lying in a network of shining capillaries over the whole moor. When Philip galloped the colt across apparently dry going, the flying hooves sent up spray in their wake. Day after day the mists came, thin and sinister. Philip was familiar with their tricks, their legerdemain with landmarks and their distortion of size and distance. He continued to ride every day regardless of the weather, knowing that soon, when the snows came, he would be stopped.

One day early in November, rain fell in an unfaltering deluge; the boy stayed indoors reading until after lunch when it slackened and finally died away in desultory spasms. A little after four o'clock, he caught the colt, bridled it and set off for a quick ride before dusk. He took it up the hill past the Forest Inn and on to the top road that led out past Combestone Tor to Holne. From here he went through the gate and across Mrs. Coaker's field to the open moor beyond. The colt was keen and plunged once or twice in high spirits, so where the track broadened out to climb the long swell of the hill towards Aune Head he squeezed it forward into a canter. A light rain had started up again and the fine drops were flicking at his face as they went into the wind; when they had passed the first of the ruined buildings he brought the colt back to him, riding in with his seat as the moorman had taught him. As it came down to a walk he saw the mist coming towards them, seeming to send out exploratory tendrils like antennae as it crept across the rolling ground. He halted the pony and waited for it to come, curious to see if it was going to be as thick as it appeared to be from a distance. One moment he was watching the rocks and bilberry clumps steadily disappearing and the next moment he was isolated — completely — in a sea of swirling mist. It was a thick one all right; it was one of the worst that Philip had ever known, but near to home as he was he remained quite unruffled and turned the colt back the way they had come. As they moved steadily through the drenched vegetation Philip looked around him in

144

wonder; the mist seemed to vary constantly in aspect: now so thick as to appear solid and then suddenly translucent and seeming to glow with an unearthly opalescence in the fading light. The thudding of the colt's hooves had a muffled, distorted quality and the only other sound was the swish-swish of the heather as droplets of water scattered in showers of pearls. A figure loomed up to one side: The colt jerked to a halt and snorted at it in sudden fear, but it became a rock standing up at a steep angle like a menhir; the colt walked on again but warily now, its ears moving constantly.

They were moving through deep heather; Philip looked about him for some semblance of a path but there was none. The mist was so thick that even the ground ahead of the colt's forefeet showed dimly and he could see nothing three or four paces ahead. Not at all disturbed, he turned towards the left, reckoning that he had strayed off to the right and that this manoeuvre would bring him back on to the path. However, after a little while had elapsed and still there was no path, he began to worry a little; he was aware, too, that what light there was would soon be gone. The ground began to break up and become uneven; rocks showed now in increasing numbers, hard to see in the dying light.

Suddenly the boy realised that they were going downhill again. Knowing that this must be wrong he turned the colt's head uphill and urged it into a trot: It went unwillingly in stiff, hesitant strides, snorting with fear. The mist was like a cocoon, like a shroud: It deadened sound and

145

set the boy's sense of balance awry so that he found it hard to stay on the colt's back as it plunged through the deep heather, leaping and stumbling over ghostly boulders. Something loomed . . . a blankness, a nothingness . . . not knowing what he did Philip threw his weight back and to one side wrenching the colt's head round viciously. He felt a lurch and a scramble, the sickening feeling as the animal's forehand began to fall and then recovered, fighting insanely for balance and the firm ground — after what seemed an age the colt flung back and stood trembling in every inch of its body, staring in terror at the mine shaft into which they had almost fallen. In the spectral light it was a pool of blackness. Philip felt the blood drain from his head and he slid from the colt's back and squatted on the ground for a moment until the faintness receded. He fumbled on the ground for a stone, found one, and then carefully tossed it into the old shaft: It shone once, dull and smooth, before disappearing; there were long seconds before the faint sound of its fall echoed back.

All at once he seemed to recover his awareness. Rising swiftly he mounted the colt and looked desperately round to determine his direction. He knew where he was: He knew the mine shafts and the old engine house and the other ruined remnants of the tin miners, but he had no idea of his bearings. Uphill flashed again into his mind and he sent the pony forward at a fast walk, not daring to go faster lest the ground open again beneath their feet. There was no more light, yet it was by no means dark; the mist was

146

visible, tangible it seemed; shining with an un-earthly radiance like a glow-worm's light . . . cold and deadly. He became aware of sounds: his breathing and that of the colt, the thud and crackle of the hooves, the dripping everywhere of moisture. He reined in and sat tensely, strain-ing to hear . . . he felt cold as it came again: the thin impossibly distant sound of a horn. Something within him struggled to marshal reason and commonsense, but it was no use: Fear was riding his shoulders now as he rode the colt and it ran down his body like an electric current, jolting the animal beneath him into sudden flight. The colt ran and again the thin wail of the hunting horn sounded, seeming to come from the sky, ahead and behind at one and the same time. A name burned in the boy's mind: Dewer . . . Dewer the wild huntsman, who hunts men's souls on the moor with a pack of phantom hounds . . . Dewer, the gaunt, the black-hooded and cloaked . . . Dewer, the relentless . . . "No — it's n-not!" he shouted aloud. His voice was swal-lowed as the colt galloped on across the endless heather and the hunting horn sounded again — louder still — mournful and pitiless, menacing and everywhere in the invisible sky. He started to shout, tattered fragments of sound like sobs; the colt was mad, its blood poisoned by the fear that coursed from the boy's limbs. Philip swayed and clutched at the flying mane; his eyes closed and he felt his mind beginning to withdraw from the nightmare that enveloped him . . . felt obliv-ion lapping at the borders of his consciousness . . . willed it to advance and take him out of

147

the nightmare of pounding hooves and the eld-ritch keening of the terrible horn as it echoed out of the sky and shivered through the swirling mist. But another sound came, forcing itself to his notice; it came again, faint and muffled by distance: "Philip!"

His eyes opened wide; the nightmare faded and was gone. Instantly he took hold of the pony and pulled it together, slowing it down. He shouted exultantly: "Here!"

It came again, faint but clear: "Philip!"

He recognised the moorman's voice and laughed aloud in his relief: "Oh . . . thank you . . ." his voice broken; then he shouted again: "Here! Here I am!"

"Philip! Over here, lad!"

He slowed the colt to a walk and patted its neck; he could feel that it was still trembling violently and the dark, metallic smell of its sweat filled his nostrils. At last he saw the light, like a firefly in the dimness, and then the old man.

"Are you all right, lad? My, you gave us a fright! Your mother's half-crazy . . ." he talked on and the boy followed, glad of the chance to recover his composure and still his pounding heart. The old man walked at the colt's head, one hand on the nearside rein; looking down, Philip could just discern the path that led across the last forty yards to Mrs. Coaker's field and the road. The moorman was still talking:

". . . and when it got dark that was too much altogether, so out I came. I could hardly find the road it was so bad."

He turned to look at Philip:

"Did you hear the horn?" he asked brightly. Philip felt a clutch of fear at his heart.

"W-what horn?" he whispered.

"This one, of course," the old man replied and pulled a hunting horn out of his pocket.

"I was blowing it a little while ago: thought it would carry farther than my voice. I was having fun, I can tell you; started off with the 'Gone-away' but I got out of breath so I went on to the 'Gone-to-earth'; didn't use up nearly so much — "

He stopped abruptly as laughter welled up out of the boy's mouth, and stood looking at him in amazement. Philip was laughing silently, leaning forward over the colt's neck and clutching his stomach with one hand; as he writhed helplessly, tears streamed down his face until it was impossible any longer to identify his emotion. The old man shook his head slowly.

"What's the —"

But Philip could not tell him: not then. Later, as they walked down the road side by side, the pony following close behind, he told the old man of his flight from the wild huntsman. Mrs. Ransome, standing fearfully at the front door, was startled by the sound of laughter coming clearly through the swirling darkness as the muffled footsteps approached.

When Philip went to bed that night he still smiled to think of it, remembering the laughter he had shared with the moorman.

Alone in the drifting mist and the dripping darkness, the white colt was still trembling as the terrible horn echoed on and on through the long night and the nightmare congealed like ice in its bloodstream.

149

With the arrival of December, the winter seemed to gather momentum; long-delayed by the spell of fine weather, the autumn had lingered as if apologetically for a week or two and had finally faded, washed away by the swollen rivers and the mists. Now winter was quickening the pace; the rains began to thin; sudden sharp frosts surprised the water-logged ground into a white blush and there were days of brilliant cold sunshine when the madder-brown and purple of the moors seemed to glow.

The colt had grown a heavy coat by now and sweated easily so they went mostly at a walk, the boy well wrapped against the cold wind. One day he heard the faint note of a hunting horn, but it was the foxhounds; he saw them in the distance, the scarlet coats winking in the fitful sunlight. The colt too had heard the horn and was trembling violently, its ears pricked sharply towards the moving specks of colour near the horizon. Soon he could hear the clamour of the hounds as they approached him and his blood stirred and leapt as they swept past him, strung out, noses down, tongues hanging, with their indescribable pack-voice, mournful and dangerous. The colt stood like a statue as they passed, its eyes following their course; then the horn spoke again with its metallic "twang" thrilling through the clear air; at this sound the colt began to prance and sidle and as the horsemen approached, following the lone huntsman on his big grey, Philip could contain himself no longer: neither his own mounting excitement nor the colt's as it plunged and snorted. The field was in three or four distinct groups, following their own line across the difficult country that lay over Tor Royal towards Princetown.

Philip followed the lone huntsman as he in turn followed in the wake of the screaming hounds, their cry blown back in gusts to the boy's ears as he struggled to keep his seat on the excited pony. Although neither so big nor so fast as most of the horses in the field, the colt had the advantage of its life on the moors; its unshod hooves flew unerringly across the awkward going, as it constantly changed legs, shortening and extending its stride to maintain its speed through the heather and bilberry; occasionally it jumped a gorse bush or even leapt on to a flat boulder that lay across its path and off the other side. They arrived at the first stone walls, near Princetown. Philip saw horses and riders silhouetted momentarily against the sky as they jumped them, others swerving violently as they refused, then his attention was claimed as he approached

151

his first obstacle: a Dartmoor wall of grey, round-ed stones. He had seen the huntsman take it in his stride, but he had never learned how to jump and was unsure of the colt's reaction. A place caught his eyes where stones had tumbled and lay in a heap across a gap; certain now, he turned towards it. As they approached the colt pricked its ears at the place, slowed down and scrambled neatly across, flinging itself forward again across the smooth turf of the newtake.

The boy's heart rose at the drumming of the hooves on the short grass and the singing of the wind in his ears. He felt as though they had grown wings and were soaring above green clouds. Through an open gate and on again, the hunt drawing away from him a little, the colt lathered black yet still straining forward, fleet and sure. A great upstanding wall checked him at last; there was no gap here and the gate refused to open. For a little while he tried to find a way around but the hunt had gone, had disappeared like smoke; only a couple of distant figures re-peatedly trying to jump a wall on horses that would not face it, exhausted perhaps. At last he gave up and made his way home across the moor. The whole way back the colt was scanning the horizon eagerly, champing at the bit and giving impatient little shakes of its head. Even when he released it in the paddock behind the moorman's cottage, it trotted immediately to the top corner and stood as if frozen, its head high, its eyes, ears, and nose testing the wind, before swinging violently and galloping like a lunatic down the field and back to its vantage point, repeating the process over and over.

That evening Philip went to see the moorman; he had to tell him about the hunt. The old man listened, smiling at the boy's evident excitement as he tripped over his words, remembering the rushing wind and the cry of the hounds. He remembered too his own young heart lifting at the sight of rows of black cut-and-laid fences standing menacingly across the beautiful turf of the shires; the throwing away of cigars and the ramming down of silk hats at the echoing yell of the view-holler: the sharp competition amongst the Subalterns from the Remount Depot at Melton where he was stationed. His eyes lost their faraway look and returned to the boy as he realized: something is worrying him. Philip had finished his breathless description of the run in which he had taken part and was now looking preoccupied, frowning slightly and searching for words. The old man waited and at last the boy spoke.

"W-what w-w-were the hounds chasing? I m-mean, they were chasing a f-fox, w-weren't they?"

"Yes, they were. Must have been a stranger, too, the way he was running."

The boy thought again, plucking unseeingly at the sleeve of his jersey, still frowning.

"B-but . . . is it c-cruel?"

"What makes you ask that?" the moorman said, puzzled.

"I w-was reading about it in the n-newspaper. It s-said that p-people who go hunting are cruel."

"Ah." The old man understood and he sighed. All the old arguments swam through his mind: the embittered altercations with friends, stale

153

dogma and erroneous attacks, his own anger at
the prejudiced propaganda put out against hunting; and what use was all that to the boy? None.

"Look, Philip; they say that it's bloodthirsty
to hunt the fox, right?"

The boy nodded.

"Then *you* tell *me,* what did you feel when you
joined with the hunt today?"

"W-well, it w-was exciting. And — well, the
g-galloping and — and — I wanted to j-jump a
wall, b-but we haven't p-practised, and . . ." he
broke off, his eyes shining. The old man smiled.

"And how about the fox — did you want them
to catch him?"

"Oh no. I d-didn't really think about the f-fox."
The boy looked surprised. "In f-fact, I th-think
I was on his side —" He stopped and then asked
anxiously: "— but that's silly isn't it?"

"No, Philip," the old man replied gently, almost dreamily, "that isn't silly. That's the answer
to the whole thing if they did but know it."

The boy was filled now with the ambition to
follow the hunt and leap the stone walls. Before
falling asleep at night he would dream of mara-
thon runs across the moor on his white hunter.

The moorman found himself again being
drawn into almost daily contact with the boy as
he demanded jumping lessons and information
about hunting. Again, bad weather found the two
of them in the old man's study looking at books
from his extensive sporting collection. He warned

154

the boy that it would be a long preparation, that he must not expect to be able to go hunting on his own until the following year, that he and the pony both had a lot to learn. All of this the boy accepted and pressed for more tuition. The old man resigned himself to the situation and began to school the two of them whenever the weather permitted.

It was the weather that put a stop to it all, in the end. Frosts had been recurring, sharper and longer, and days had been clear and hard with the mercury around freezing-point from dawn until dusk. The colt still lived in the paddock. Every day the boy took it a quarter of a bale of hay and broke the ice on the trough.

"No, don't bring him in," Hugh Otterburn had said, "he's a moorland pony, he'll be better where he is. See that he has enough to eat and that he can get at his water, give him a shelter from the wind and he'll be happier and healthier where he is than in any stable."

One evening, after a day of leaden skies and fitful gusts of wind, snow started to fall. Softly at first in fine flakes, then in larger flakes and finally in great fluffy discs the size of a half-crown, the snow fell all through the night. The next morning it was lying over the moor in an even blanket and it was still falling. When Philip went to the paddock to see the pony he was startled to see how yellow its coat looked against the purity of the new snow. All that day and all through the night and the next day as well, the great soft flakes fell silently on the moor. Although it lay deep, the roads were still open to those

155

vehicles with the basic design that made them function in adverse conditions. Examples of the other kind began to appear by the roadsides, in the ditches and slewed across hills in increasing numbers. So far, it was fun: Children played and gambolled in the unaccustomed softness, while animals found no difficulty in obtaining their food from beneath it. But the third night changed all that. Before midnight a wind arose; gently at first; whistling mournfully around the houses and across the bleak tors, it gathered strength and direction and became a howling force that assaulted everything that dared to stand against its will. It picked up the loosely packed snow from the open places and carried it for miles, hurling it finally against any obstruction so that drifts developed rapidly against every wall, every bank, and over every hollow place. Then, when the drift had built up to the top of the obstruction the wind was able to scream unhindered over it, triumphant in its destructive power. So strong was it that the moor seemed to smoke as the finely powdered snow was whipped up and carried to its next position. The Great Blizzard was on.

The wind blew flat and deadly for days. Philip had to fight his way to the field to give the colt its hay; each day it stood in the same place, under the wall: its back into the wind, its head down, ice crystals all over its back and quarters where the snow had thawed and frozen again. Turning to fight his way back home again Philip caught the full force of the wind in the face.

The animals stuck it out grimly: collecting into groups and seeking shelter if any was near, standing huddled for warmth or burrowing beneath the snow, according to their ilk. Birds began to die.

On the afternoon of the fourth day, two prisoners broke away from a working party returning to the prison; they were swallowed up almost immediately in the poor visibility. Warders who set out to track them found that they had divided. Forming two parties, they continued to follow the fast-disappearing tracks. Two hours later, three warders found one of the prisoners lying in deep snow, only semiconscious. On their return to the prison, all four were treated for frostbite. The other party had no luck: The tracks died out completely and they returned to the prison. One of them reported that before the tracks had been lost they had become very irregular, as though the man had been staggering. Two days later there had been no report of a break-in anywhere on Dartmoor and the roads were impassable, so the missing prisoner was given up for dead. It was confidently expected that his body would appear when the thaw came.

There were newspaper reports that foxes were hunting in packs and pulling down healthy sheep. Town dwellers reading these items over their breakfasts murmured in surprise at the barbarities of nature. Those people who knew their countryside dismissed the reports as the nonsense that they were.

By the time the wind began to drop, six days later, there were already emergencies enough to keep the R.A.F. helicopters busy all day, clattering across the white emptiness to isolated farms

157

and small holdings with supplies, and returning with sick people and expectant mothers. The wind died away and the freeze set in. Trodden or packed snow was like glass; deep snow became deadly with a frozen crust through which a man could fall into a drift ten feet deep from which it would be impossible to escape. Everything was white and still, and deadly cold.

There was an ammil, too. On December 21st a fog came down over the village and the surrounding moor. There was no breath of wind, nothing to break the even, slowly drifting greyness. Philip, returning from the field just before dusk found his coat covered in countless spicules of ice that crackled when the material moved; seconds later he was startled when he caught a glimpse of his face in a mirror: His hair was glistening with the same armour. The temperature remained just below freezing point all day; with the coming of nightfall it plummeted to 24° F., eight degrees of frost. In the morning the ammil was on and people woke up to a scene from fairyland. . . .

Every twig on the trees, every smallest blade of grass, every pine needle, every sprig of heather had a suit of transparent ice. Gorse bushes made fantastic shapes and branches fell, scattering shattered fragments of ice that tinkled down onto the frozen snow. Strong twigs had a sheath of ice up to an inch thick; fine blades of grass had the merest film of ice, so that they hardly bent with the additional weight. The sun was bright in a blue sky and where it shone the ice pendents became diamonds, flashing the colours

158

of the rainbow, sparkling impossibly as a breath
of wind set the bejewelled twigs into motion. A
holly tree just off the road outside Hexworthy
drew a steady stream of admirers: its strong green
and brilliant red set the ice glowing, so that children stood open-mouthed in wonder. Towards
the end of the afternoon the magic was fading;
everywhere there were the little sounds of dissolution as the ice melted away. When dawn
came on the following morning disappointed children searched in vain for a single necklace of
glittering ice. So ephemeral had it been that even
the memory of the ammil would become transient
and dreamlike . . . yet many years later, when
these same children have grown up and married
and become accustomed to things, a recurrence of
the same conditions will halt them in their tracks
and their minds will fly back over the years and
grasp just a little fragment of the childish wonder
that enchanted them when they saw their first
ammil.

It was two days after that, on December 24th,
that the old man and the boy were called upon
to help John Brookshaw, up at Sherberton. Two
days before the blizzard had struck, John's ponies
and black Galloway cattle had begun to arrive in
from the moor; by the time it started most of his
stock were in or around the farm, but he had
noticed that one of Diana's favourite mares, old
Cherry, was missing with her foal and a few
other ponies. While the gale blew they could do
nothing but wait and hope, and as soon as the
wind dropped they began to search for the missing group. It is the old ponies who die in hard

weather: the very old and the very young. Diana was anxious to find them and fetch them in if possible lest the bad spell continue. They searched as well as they could, on foot and in the Land-Rover, John driving it without mercy across the moors in conditions undreamed of by its designers.

At last, two days before Christmas, they found the ponies. They were in a deep gully in Brownberry plantation, where they had sheltered from the terrible wind. When it finally dropped they found themselves trapped, kept in by steep, slippery walls on three sides and an impassable drift on the fourth. Diana had seen them from a distance and did not know how Cherry had fared, but she recognised some of the ponies as belonging to the same group as the old mare, so she and John decided to try to get them out the following day. The moorman heard about it from old Reg in the Forest Inn that evening and telephoned to offer his services and those of the boy.

The next morning the Land-Rover arrived to pick them up and the five of them set off with John at the wheel, the back of the Land-Rover cluttered with spades and ropes. He approached the wood across the high ground; at first they drove through fields and the going was easy, but once on the moor the vehicle started to buck and swerve like a living thing. Once they rebounded from a rock and old Reg hit his head hard on the roof, landing with a crash on the shaft of a spade. He swore fiercely as he recovered his seat, then paused, rubbing his head tenderly and muttering audibly:

160

"Buggered if I shan't brek my bliddy neck if I dew that again! or brek my bliddy tail — one or t'other!" John looked at the moorman who smiled back rather wanly, hanging on with both hands to the bar beneath the windscreen. At last they arrived at the top edge of the wood and clambered out, reaching in for the spades and a few head-collars.

"We'll leave the ropes there till we know whether we'll need 'em or not," said John, and they set off carrying a spade apiece. At first the going was easy, the snow fairly thin beneath the close-woven canopy of the conifers, but as they began to breast the hill, the trees became thinner and great outcrops of rock appeared. The snow became steadily deeper and as the ground broke up it was impossible to be sure that the next step would not be into a deep drift. Once Philip half fell and recovered and once old Reg disappeared completely from view to be pulled out by John, struggling and blaspheming terribly. But they made progress and finally arrived at the beginning of the gully. It was full of untouched snow, stretching smoothly from one side to the other. There was no sound, apart from their own harsh breathing.

"Must be farther up," said Diana.

They worked carefully up the side of the gully and came across the ponies only thirty or forty yards farther on, standing in a tight group. They looked up at their rescuers with expressions of comical surprise and a few of them whickered in anticipation, their breath condensing as it left their nostrils. Diana looked over the group; there were fourteen of them. She saw Cherry's foal immediately, but missed the mare. Again she checked them over, one by one, but there was no mistake: Cherry was not among them.

"She might have got separated from them," John said, putting a hand on her shoulder.

"Yes," she replied, but already she knew. From a little way down the gully Reg called out:

"I reckon us can dig they pawnies out down yur." They moved down to where he stood, almost hidden within his clothes, his blue eyes blinking earnestly at each one of them in turn.

"I think you're right, Reg," John said, "we should be able to get them up this slope. Once they're out it'll be plain sailing back to Sherberton."

They began to dig then, slowly and carefully, tossing the light snow away from the hillside. Even though they did not hurry there was a lot of snow to shift and soon Philip was flushed with exertion and sweating freely inside his warm clothes. He glanced at the moorman and was worried by what he saw: The old man seemed to be gritting his teeth as though in pain. Old Reg was in the van of the party, his arms going like pistons, his face a deep scarlet against the snow; as he worked he muttered and gasped, and cursed each time he struck a rock or stumbled over a hidden root. Diana worked quietly and said nothing.

It took them nearly three hours to clear away enough snow to get the ponies out. They were standing in a clearing of trampled snow, stained with their droppings. Bare patches on the sides of the gully showed where they had been able to clear away the snow and get at the vegetation beneath, but it had been very little and they were hungry. The ponies had all been handled and even halter-broken and did not object when they were approached. While the three men discussed how best to get them back to Sherberton, Diana wandered a little way up on the gully. When Philip followed her, a few minutes later, he found her kneeling in the snow uncovering something. He approached her slowly and looked over her shoulder. It was Cherry. Strangely enough the sight of death like this did not shock or frighten him. Diana had cleared away some of the snow and Cherry lay there, her forelegs tucked in as though she were dozing in the summer grass, her muzzle resting lightly on the ground. She was covered in a layer of ice and through it her eyes showed softly. They looked at her for a little while, breathing quietly, the girl kneeling, the boy standing at her shoulder. Without looking up Diana spoke, as if to herself.

"That's all right then, old lady; that's all right. It wasn't too bad, was it? It was quick."

Dreamily she stroked the cheek through its sheath of ice.

"And you've got a good foal too. He's just round the corner, and he'll be right as rain in a day or two. Looks just like you used to when you were his age."

Philip felt the tears running down his cheeks. Diana looked up and saw him, saw his tears. She reached up and took his hand.

163

"Kneel down here, Philip. By me."

He did so. She let go of his hand and looked again at the sleeping form beneath its blanket of ice.

"There's no need to be unhappy. Look at me, I'm not unhappy."

He looked at her: Her face was calm and radiant.

"Now that I've found her, I needn't worry any more; I know that she's all right now. If I hadn't found her I'd have worried lest she were in pain or suffering somewhere where I couldn't get to her. Do you see? Dying like this is as easy as falling asleep for an old pony. One minute they're alive — the next minute the heart just stops. That's all. Look how she's lying, Philip: See how relaxed she is, and how her muzzle is just resting on the ground as if she's dozing off?" Under the influence of her quiet voice, the boy's tears dried. He sensed her quiet acceptance of life and death, her understanding of the necessary cycle, and a strange joy welled up within him and shone from his eyes. She looked at him again.

"Yes. Yes, you understand now."

Suddenly she seemed to remember who he was, realised that he was the pale-faced boy who could not speak to anyone but the old man. Looking deep into his eyes she turned towards him and put her hands on his shoulders. When she spoke to him it was with the same soft voice as that with which she had spoken to the dead pony and the boy felt her words sinking into his consciousness:

164

"Philip, I know you can't answer me, but I want to tell you something . . . from all of us. You're going to be all right, do you understand? I know it. We all know it. You're going to be quite all right. We've watched you getting better every day, and I want you to know that we all care, Philip. We all care. Do you understand what I'm trying to tell you?"

He nodded silently, his eyes shining — not trying to speak and anyway unspeakably happy. Then voices broke in on his thoughts and the men were there.

Philip took in very little of the walk back to Sherberton. He, the moorman, and Diana each led a pony; the rest of the little band followed dutifully. John and Reg went back over the top to retrieve the Land-Rover.

The boy was lost in a soft glow of wonder: You who live in daily contact with other people, who employ without thought the priceless gift of communication with your fellow human beings, you cannot know — unless you dream it — the effect upon the boy of those few moments when Diana Brookshaw had spoken words straight into his opened soul.

It so happened that their route back took them almost over the spot where Lady had fallen to earth and died; and from there retraced exactly where they had last been together, the three of them, that blustering September afternoon. Yet Philip did not even realise where they were, so exalted was he.

Strange how the pain engendered by the death of a beloved animal should be washed out, ex-

165

punged completely by another death. But no more strange, really, than flowers growing from soil wherein lie countless bodies in constant dissolution. Life springing joyfully again out of death, everywhere and all the time: the eternal miracle.

The following morning the boy awoke as though to his first Christmas Day.

CHAPTER X

O N CHRISTMAS DAY the moorman came to Philip's home for a turkey dinner. Afterwards he settled into an armchair with a glass of Grand Armagnac, expecting to stay there for quite some time; before long, however, he began to feel dizzy and his throat ached, so he excused himself and returned home. Walking along the road back to his cottage he had to stop twice and lean against the wall that ran by the roadside. The next morning he was quite definitely ill. At seven-thirty he got up, feeling awful, made himself a mug of sweet tea and returned to bed. When Philip called in after seeing to the pony, at about 11 A.M., the old man called down for him to go up to the bedroom. The boy was shocked at what he saw: the moorman looked ten years older and his voice was a mere croak.

"Just a cold, lad. Or a bit of 'flu perhaps. Nothing to worry about."

But the boy was worried. Back at home again

he told his mother. After lunch Mrs. Ransome walked along to the moorman's cottage, opened the back door and called out: "Colonel! Colonel Forster!"

He had been asleep but he woke up and called to her, hoarsely, to come up. By the time she left again she had given him two hot water bottles, had telephoned the doctor and asked him to call in, and finally had made him a small bowl of bread and milk; this last request had surprised her, but the old man cherished a life-long passion for sweet bread and milk, and it was the only form of nourishment that he could face, feeling as he did. Towards the evening he noticed that breathing was slightly painful and when the doctor at last arrived he quickly diagnosed bronchitis.

"I hear you were digging ponies out of snow drifts the other day," he said breezily.

The moorman nodded, unwilling to use his voice.

"Serves you damn well right, then," the doctor said cheerfully. "You should know better at your age." The old man smiled grimly and held his peace.

They worked out a *modus operandi* to look after him: Five days a week the "daily" would spend the morning there, seeing to his needs and cleaning up wherever necessary. In the evening, around five o'clock, Mrs. Ransome would go along and cook him a broth, or boiled fish, before going back to prepare supper for her husband and Philip. At the weekends she would do the morning spell as well. When told all this the old man tried to protest but he was too weak, and anyway, it would have had no effect. At last Philip's mother had a chance to repay some of the old man's generosity, and she was happy to do so. As for the boy, he spent nearly all the time at the cottage. When the moorman was awake he would call down and Philip would make a pot of tea and carry it up to the bed-room. Then they would talk or look at a book together. Because the old man found talking pain-ful, Philip made more and more of the conversa-tion. Absorbed and relaxed at the same time, he spoke with increasing ease. Sometimes he would talk quietly, almost to himself, and the old man would realise with a start that the boy was hardly even stammering. When Philip's mother arrived, he would smile up at her and help her carry the meal upstairs when it was ready. They became so close in their mutual guardianship of the old man that she hardly noticed that her son was still unable to speak when he looked at her and smiled his slow smile.

One evening during the first week in January Barry telephoned: Mrs. Ransome took the call. Barry was momentarily nonplussed at the female voice.

"I wanted to speak to Colonel Lane-Forster, have I got the right number?"

"Yes you have, but I'm afraid he's ill; he won't be able to speak to you."

"He's ill?" Barry was shocked into silence. Mrs.

Ransome, thinking that they had been cut off, said "Hello?" Barry answered, "Yes, I'm here. Look, how bad is he? I mean, he's not badly ill, is he?"

"Well . . ." she hesitated, "Yes, I suppose he is really. He's got bronchitis rather severely and his heart isn't too good either. Can I be of any help?"

There was another silence before Barry spoke again.

"Excuse me, are you a relative of the Colonel's or something?"

"No, just a neighbour."

"Well, can you tell me, if I were to come down tomorrow, could I see him? I mean, will he be able to . . .?"

"Oh yes, I should think so. He can't talk very much, in fact hardly at all, but I'm sure you could see him if you wanted to. Who shall I say . . .?"

"Barry — Barry Holliday. Would you tell him that I'll be calling to see him tomorrow at about" — a pause — "just after lunch?" She had realised suddenly who it was and was flustered, but Barry thanked her and rang off immediately. When she told the old man, minutes later, his eyes blazed suddenly although he did not move and a smile twisted his mouth.

The next day when Barry arrived the house was quiet. After knocking gently on the door he tried the handle and found it unlocked. He passed

170

through to the bottom of the stairs and called up softly: "Colonel?"

He heard a croak from above and climbed the stairs to the old man's bedroom. Wordlessly they clasped hands, the old man's grip so weak that Barry was again shocked. He sat down on a chair by the bed and they regarded each other. The moorman tried to smile.

"Well —" he wheezed.

"That's enough," Barry said, "you sound like . . ." he searched for a simile but gave up and smiled: "anyway, don't try to talk."

The old man nodded; his eyes were steady on Barry's and the young man sensed the question. He looked down at the floor and clasped his hands, searching for words: "Colonel, I . . . I feel so bad about all this — I had no idea you were ill and anyway . . ." he broke off for a moment, then seemed to gather strength; he looked up and met the old man's gaze:

"I should have written. I should have written long ago. At first I didn't want to, I was too upset; and then later on, when I got over it, I just didn't seem to get around to it. I meant to — time and time again — but just never got around to it; I'm sorry."

The old man laid a hand on Barry's sleeve for a moment and struggled to say something:

"Forget it," then smiled his twisted smile again, but Barry was shaking his head unhappily: "I just didn't realize. . . ."

The old man waved his hand slowly across in front of him in a gesture of wiping-out, of complete effacement, and when Barry smiled he nodded his head, satisfied.

"How is Philip coming along?" Barry asked; the moorman gave the thumbs-up sign.

"Good," Barry said, and they were silent for a little while in the warmth of the room. There was so much that the moorman wanted to know, and after a little while Barry told him his news: He had not found another hawk but he had been busy in another direction and had become engaged. Again the old man smiled as he thought: no wonder he forgot to write!

Barry went on: "Luckily I'll still be able to keep a hawk — two, in fact — Jan wants one herself; so I've applied for another peregrine through the club and I've got my eye on a pair of kestrels — I think I know where they'll nest and that'll take care of Jan." He smiled: "It'll be like old times."

He talked on in this vein for some time, the old man nodding and occasionally asking a question in a combination of words and signs. Just after four o'clock they heard quick footsteps coming up to the house; Barry looked enquiringly at the old man who replied painfully: "Philip."

Barry spoke quickly: "Colonel, can I go and have a word with him — just to tell him that everything's all right about Lady? I mean, it won't upset him or anything, will it?"

The moorman shook his head and motioned to Barry to go and get on with it. When Philip saw the strange face he turned away sharply and went to leave, but Barry called to him by name and he stood arrested, his face averted, but listening. Barry had the same instinctive understanding as the moorman and Diana Brookshaw and he spoke gently: "Philip, my name's Barry and I used to own Lady —"

At the mention of the little kestrel Philip made a sharp movement and closed his eyes but Barry went on quietly and insistently: "I want you to know something: I want you to know that I'm glad Lady came here to live with you because you gave her such a good home and took such good care of her. . . ."

Philip looked at him once, asking wordlessly: But —?

Barry went on: "There was an accident, that's all, Philip. And believe me, it wasn't your fault; hawks die so easily of one thing or the other. It could have been the day after she came back to me instead of the day before. Do you see?" Philip nodded, his face averted as before.

"So you won't worry about it, will you? Promise?"

Again the boy nodded and went to leave but Barry said: "And one more thing, Philip; the Colonel is very ill — well, you know that already — but you will look after him, won't you? He's such a good man and he's done so much for me, I'll feel much better if I know that you're looking after him."

For the second time Philip looked at him and this time he smiled quickly and nodded; Barry smiled back and said: "Thanks."

Afterwards he said to the old man: "I think I can see why you're so fond of him . . . I can't explain it, but I think I can understand; he makes you *want* to help him, doesn't he?"

He had to leave almost immediately; he had

173

managed to get leave of absence for the day but would have to clock in the following morning for the early shift. Driving away towards Moreton-hampstead he knew that he had done the right thing in making the journey and that an old wound was finally healed. But he was desperately worried about the moorman: He knew that the old man was very ill.

Even though he had only met him once Barry had received the same impression from Philip as had Diana and the moorman: the conviction that it was just a matter of time before he achieved normality. As with the frozen moor around them, the thaw had to come.

It came to the moor first. On the morning of January 6th the long process began. Water started to run, snow to slide in heaps from the roofs, leaving bare grey patches that shone dully beneath the low, softening sky. The drifts began to recede infinitesimally, although some were so deep that snow lay in hollows on the high moors well into June. The attention of the newspapers, which had turned from weather conditions to the international situation, was again focused upon the moor as thousands of tons of snow and ice turned to water and dripped, trickled, ran, rushed, roared, and thundered down towards the sea. Floods! screamed the headlines. There were floods in the middle of Exeter, on Newton Abbot racecourse, and over hundreds of acres of low-lying farmland in the south. Lynton and Lynmouth came in for the usual packet and old Reg was forced to make a blasphemous detour to the Forest Inn when he found the fishermen's bridge across the Swincombe washed away. All over the moor the animals stood negatively, waiting. In the snow they could scrape for food and sleep warm; in the wet they were miserable. The shaggy scotch sheep that had bustled cheerfully through the Great Blizzard and the freeze-up which followed now stood glumly on the high ground, moving restlessly from one fastidious foot to the other, while the whole moor seemed to move in one unbroken sheet of water towards the lower country to the south.

The moorman's illness took a turn for the worse; his temperature rose and he became feverish; speech became impossible and breathing was a constant agony. Between periods of delirium, when he seemed to float on a current of distant pain, he would lie exhausted. During these periods of lucidity he had time to reassess his relationship with Philip; he came to realise how completely their roles had intermingled.

Philip began to ride again. At first the colt was unruly, having been without exercise for almost a month, so the boy decided to give it a good long ride on the second day to give it sufficient work to quieten it down.

On the morning of January 11th he set out with a packet of biscuits, stolen from the larder, hidden in his pocket. The temperature was in the high forties; the moor smelt damp and hugely fertile, and dirty looking snow still lay in patches everywhere. He started out towards Aune Head and one of the loneliest parts of Dartmoor, where the Aune, or Avon, rises and sets out on its long journey. After less than a mile he found himself passing the old tin workings; he wandered amongst them for a while trying to find the mine-shaft that had nearly claimed him in the mist, but it was impossible and soon he moved on. The character of the moor was changing; it was becoming wider and more level, although its main feature was still visible: a great bowl of peat, miles across, surrounded by low hills. In the bowl were patches of brilliant green and dark brown . . . the whole area was a mass of bogs, but the higher ground was relatively dry. The colt still had a coat like a polar bear so Philip kept it down to a walk most of the time, although when they came to a stretch of dry turf he allowed it to canter collectedly across it, the colt fighting for its head but unable to get its own way. Past Aune Head, Philip began to sweep round to the right: He had decided to go back by Fox Tor because he had never seen Childe's Tomb, although the moorman had told him the legend attached to it. It stands on a bleak, open hillside, miles from the nearest road; below it and to either side are some of the deepest bogs on the moor, known collectively as Fox Tor Mire. Philip did not worry about getting into a bog: He had absolute confidence in the colt's ability to keep them both out of trouble. Generally speaking, ponies —

especially ponies bred on the moor — seem to have a sixth sense where these soft spots are concerned; they will usually refuse to go forward if dangerous ground lies ahead. However, sometimes circumstances conspire to circumvent a pony's natural caution.

Descending the long incline towards where he knew Childe's Tomb to be, Philip felt the colt still exuberant beneath him; seeing level going ahead he urged it to a canter. It went strongly but sensibly so he let it out to a gallop. It was still going sensibly when a hare got up from right beneath its feet and jinked to one side, its ears flat back and then raised as it made off. The colt exploded with a squeal into a series of stiff-legged bucks. The boy, bareback as always, stood not a chance and for the third time he felt himself falling. Again the horizon tilted, again the ground came up slowly to meet him, his eyes seeing and recording the fine-leaved moor grass and stalks of brown sedge. The landing was soft; he rolled twice and sat up, unperturbed — then froze in horror at what he saw.

It was like a film in slow-motion . . . or the kind of nightmare where you are trying to run away from something dreadful, only you are trying to run through deep viscous mud. . . . The pony was plunging, its momentum sending it toppling forward, its forelegs propping against ground that had no substance, while its hind legs tried desperately to engage beneath it. As the boy watched, terrified, the plunges became deeper and slower . . . as the colt came up like a great fish, its once-white coat was black and

177

glistening horribly; rearing frantically and still plunging forward, it went deeper and deeper into the mire. Philip rose to his feet and took a couple of steps forward, but he could do nothing: just stand and watch like a rabbit mesmerised by a stoat as the colt sank towards oblivion. It fought, the colt . . . its ears straining back, its eyes wide, its nostrils flared, its breath coming in great gasps of effort, it fought the unknown that clung to it and tried to drag it down . . . but the fight was costing it dear: Its sides were heaving and sweat was running dark from its neck as it struggled on, slower and lower . . . its quarters no longer showed, no longer rose like a glistening whale above the quaking, treacherous surface . . . only its head and neck reared up now like a sea-serpent, twisting and jerking as the invisible legs still fought the embrace of the terrible mud.

Then, suddenly, it seemed to give up. Philip's hand fluttered towards his mouth and his eyes stared in horror as the colt stopped struggling, but it did not happen: The head and neck stayed where they were, only the nostrils blowing in and out, in and out as the colt fought for breath. The boy tried to approach more closely but the ground shivered beneath his feet; he dropped to the ground and started to crawl, not knowing what he could do if he reached it. He got to within twenty feet of it when the earth seemed to swallow him. For a second he felt the cold slime against his face, then he too was fighting for his life: Somehow he twisted round, choking horribly, lights flickering across the blackness of his

178

closed eyes. One of his flailing hands found a tussock and clutched at it; he pulled himself towards safety, the other hand seeking and finding fresh purchase, his legs churning in desperation. When he had dragged himself clear of the horror of the mire his unwitting body carried him on for yards on to solid ground, humping across the turf like a seal, his eyes showing white in his slime-covered face. He tore up handfuls of grass and wiped insanely at his face and body, trying to rid himself of the filth that covered him. Then he was sick, agonisingly, and afterwards lay exhausted.

At last he came to his senses and sat up with a jerk; the colt had not moved. It had a strange look about it, a negative quality, as though it were waiting calmly for something to happen; it looked as though the time for fighting had gone for ever, that it would drift just as calmly into death. Painfully the boy gathered his faculties, knowing that a limit had been set on the colt's lifetime . . . that the sands of its life were running out steadily. Help, came sluggishly into his mind. I must get help. Then more urgently, I must get help! At last his limbs obeyed him: He stood up, swaying slightly, and then set off towards home, the memory of the tired, passive white head burning behind his eyes as he faced the enormous distance between himself and succour.

It took him more than two hours to cover the three and a half miles of moorland, and he was nearing exhaustion as he finally reached the road about half a mile from the village. Going down the hill he gathered momentum, his weak legs barely coping with the speed, his lungs burning and nausea gripping at his throat. He covered the last two hundred yards to the moorman's cottage and ran up the path. As he flung open the door and disappeared inside the time was just after half past one.

But this time the moorman could not help him: He was far too ill. As the boy stammered out his story the old man was not fully conscious, but at the sight of his filthy face and imploring eyes he made a terrible effort of concentration; silencing the boy with a raised hand he said, almost inaudibly:

"Tell . . . your . . . mother."

Philip stared at the old man, wide-eyed and silent; he seemed to realise for the first time how ill he was. As he stood up to go, the old man whispered:

"Can't . . . help . . . this time," his eyes looking up sadly out of his grey face.

Philip ran from the house and turned towards home. The moorman's illness and consequent helplessness had had an effect on the boy: When he arrived he had been half-crazed with fear and exhaustion, to the extent of not appreciating that the old man could be of no use to him; now he was a little calmer and was thinking clearly, although beneath the surface he was in a turmoil of agony and doubt and the colt's weary head drooping above the mire kept him constantly teetering on the edge of a black pit of despair.

When his mother saw him she could not at

180

first think of anything beyond his appearance: his clothes dark grey with the dry mud, his face streaked with the same filth. Then, by degrees, she noticed the haunted look on his face, the plea in his eyes. All this time he was leading her, pulling her by the sleeve out of the dining-room where she had been dusting, out of the house to the garden. He was pointing, now, up to the horizon, towards the west, and his mouth was working, his eyes tear-blurred. At last she caught his urgency: taking his two hands in her own she looked into his eyes and said quickly: "Philip, what is it, What is it?"

He made a sound that could have been a sob and his eyes closed for a moment, his forehead furrowed with effort.

"Philip, what's the matter? What's wrong?"

I can't, I can't! his mind screamed . . . I can't! He shut his eyes again but there was no escape. Again he saw the terrible slow-motion rolling plunges as the colt sank inexorably towards the end of all blackness and horror. He opened his eyes: his mother's eyes were full on his, he felt her love and her strength like something reaching out to touch him.

"Oh, Philip, my love, what is it?"

He saw the tears start in her eyes too. They were clinging to each other, standing like wrestlers grappling and the colt was rolling and heaving sluggishly in a nightmare of black mire.

"M-m . . . m-m . . ." He made sounds and iron bars seemed to crash down across the front of his brain, their clash echoing inside his skull: In the blackness the colt's white head was sinking . . . he could see bubbles popping viscously on the quaking surface as its nostrils went under . . . he drew a deep breath and shouted: "Oh!" as if to crash the barrier, clear the obstruction, blow the dam . . . in an impossible close-up he saw the colt's blue eyes, fey and mournful beneath their long white lashes . . . he saw the greedy mire reach up to swallow them, saw it dimple at the lower lid then leap and drag exultantly . . . he saw, he saw the perfect sky-blue eyes sink calmly down and disappear . . . for ever . . . his eyes still closed, he seemed to sag so that she had to hold him to stop him from falling, and then he was speaking.

"M-m-my pony . . . oh please, please! M-my pony!"

"What, Philip? What?"

He opened his eyes again, tears scoring fresh lines in the dirt on his cheeks: "In the m-m-mire . . . F-Fox Tor . . . oh please!"

"Your pony, it's in the mire?"

"Yes. Oh please!" Clinging to her, imploring. Suddenly she was calm. As if her whole life had led up to this point, she took over, at last her love and her strength had an adversary: The thing that was threatening her child was her enemy and she would fight it and vanquish it. Her confusion, her hesitancy, her watchfulness, all left her and she was icy calm and strong enough.

"Is it still all right?"

He nodded quickly, still holding on to her.

"Tell me exactly where it is."

"N-n-near Ch-childes — "

"Near Childe's Tomb, right. Come along."

She led him indoors, her mind working: who to call on? The Colonel was much too ill, even to give advice . . . then she remembered John Brookshaw and the rescue party on Christmas Eve. Diana answered the telephone:

"John hasn't come in for lunch yet; can I help?"

Mrs. Ransome told her what had happened.

"Whereabouts is he?" Diana asked.

"Fox Tor Mire, near Childe's Tomb."

"Oh my goodness." A short silence, then: "Look, Mrs. Ransome, just hold on. I'll go and find John. We'll be over as soon as we can. Have Philip ready because we shall need him to show us where the pony is. I don't know exactly where John is so it may take a little while to find him but we'll be there. All right?"

"Yes, thank you — "

"And tell Philip not to worry: John's always pulling ponies out of some kind of mess or another. I'll be off then — 'bye."

Philip was standing behind her, swaying as though about to faint. She caught hold of him.

"Everything's going to be all right, Philip; John will get him out for you, don't worry." He nodded.

"Now, he won't be here for at least twenty minutes or so — go and take those clothes off and put on some dry ones: you'll have to come with us, you know. Be quick and then come down here and we'll have a cup of tea while we wait. Go along."

As she filled the kettle, her hands were trembling but her mind was still and poised: She knew what had happened, knew that a barrier somewhere in his mind had given under the pressure; she could feel the joy and the exultation waiting for her; she could see the future opening out. But she would not look at it, nor savour it, nor even touch it gently with her mind. Afterwards, she thought, and went to change her clothes for the job ahead.

The Land-Rover arrived at twenty to three: John had been out shepherding a long way from the house. Mrs. Ransome, in a pair of old corduroy slacks, got into the front, next to Diana; Philip climbed into the back where Reg was sitting.

As they moved off John said: "I'm afraid we're pushed for time; we *must* get the pony out before dark, and it couldn't be in a more inaccessible place. I'm going to get as close to it as I can in the car — then, I'm afraid, we'll have to walk."

Diana spoke: "There's fairly good going to within about a mile of the place so we should make it all right."

"Pity we can't get the Rover right up to it," John said, "I can whip ponies out of bogs in a flash with this thing."

They left the road and started the long trek across the moor. They were all too busy keeping their seats to talk, beyond an occasional comment from Diana as she saw dry going ahead. Reg greeted every crashing jolt with his usual muttered curses, but when he could he peered at Philip from his deep-set blue eyes. He could not understand what was stopping — what had ever stopped — the boy from talking: He ap-

184

peared so normal. Reg's natural kindness made him yearn for contact with Philip; the barrier of the boy's silence and shyness made the old man stare sadly at him, shaking his head slowly.

In low gear they bumped, crawled, and slid across the empty moor. The sun was hidden by clouds, but it was all too low in the sky. The boy, crouching tensely in the back, watched it almost perceptibly sinking towards the dim blue line of the horizon, while in his mind the colt's tired white head slipped slowly down towards the mud.

There were patches of brilliant green around them now and sedge grew everywhere. John slipped the Land-Rover out of gear and switched the engine off; it came to a halt immediately. They clambered out and waited while the two men went to the back of the vehicle to get the necessary gear. The moor was silent and the ticking of the engine as it cooled sounded unnaturally loud in the stillness. A slight movement of air made Philip shudder. John emerged with a heavy rope round one shoulder; Reg carried a light line and two sacks. As they moved off, Diana glanced at her watch: twenty-five to four.

The clouds that massed on the horizon were suffused with a dim radiance; through breaks in the clouds above the sky was high and the colour of metal. A cold wind was getting up and all over the moor the sedge was trembling and nodding. They tramped in silence, saving their breath, Philip looked at his mother walking beside Diana, a little way ahead. He found it hard to recognise the workmanlike figure: The trousers and rubber boots made her stride like a man. When she

185

turned anxiously to see that he was all right she found him looking at her; he smiled at her briefly and she nodded back, then looked ahead again, reassured.

They saw the colt at five past four. Philip had expected to see it from a long way off and had been peering ahead with rising anxiety, but John knew better. The boy had taken the lead now, with John at his side, and was feeling the beginnings of a terrible certainty that the colt was gone when they saw it: a faint dash of white against the dim ochre and brown of the moor. Drawing up to it they could see the softer green that suggested the mire and the long dark scar of the colt's struggle into its heart. Philip felt relief at first, then noticed how objects were becoming indistinct in the fading light and colours were running into grey. He knew in his heart that the colt could not survive the night in the mire.

Twenty yards away John stopped and threw his rope down. Reg followed suit.

"Wait here a moment, I'll have a look," John said briefly and walked forward carefully. He reconnoitred the extent of the mire, and then beckoned them over to a point almost directly in front of the colt and about twenty-five feet away from it. All this time there was no movement from the white head in the mire: no flicker of eye or ear. Looking at it Philip thought suddenly of Cherry, frozen to death, lying with her muzzle resting on the ground just as the colt's muzzle was touching the surface of the mire. He opened his eyes wide to shut out the image and looked across at his mother. She was watching him and smiled, but he could not smile back: The vision of the dead mare was persisting and was slowly freezing his heart within him.

John had stripped down to the waist, a short powerful figure, seemingly unconscious of the bitterly cold wind. He tied the light line round his waist and handed the coil to Reg. Without saying a word, intent on what he was doing, he began to walk slowly towards the colt. Again Diana glanced at her watch: four fifteen. The horizon was etched darkly against a sky that flamed briefly yellow, the only colour in the whole landscape. John lurched suddenly and leaned forward, arms outspread as he sank to his knees. The movement ceased and he waded slowly forward, sinking rapidly. The blackness rose to his waist and then stopped half-way up his chest. He was holding his arms out in front pushing aside the surface carpet of sphagnum. The colt gave no sign of awareness, passive in its animal sadness. Suddenly, two yards from his goal, John seemed to topple slowly forward: as his chin sank to the surface of the mire he struck out as though swimming. There was a brief commotion, then the watchers saw him clutch the top of the colt's neck and pull himself up to it.

He remained still a moment and they could hear him gasping for breath; then he called out: "So far so good. Now chuck me that rope will you, Reg. Don't hit the pony, mind."

As the old man carefully threw the rope out it was a blur in the dimness. From where they stood they could not make out John's features as he collected up a couple of yards of the strong rope. Working up to his chest in the mire, John left the heavy rope where it was in front of him, half-submerged, and put his hands down into the bog to undo the light line from his waist. He came up with the end of it in hands that dripped blackness and tied it quickly in a bowline round the pony's neck, just behind the head.

"Here's the nasty bit," he said conversationally, then took a deep breath and ducked right under the surface. It seemed an age before he reappeared, clawing the filth ineffectually off his face with one hand, the other hand still beneath the surface. He was gasping and spitting. In a strangled voice he said, "That's the nastiest mire I've ever tasted, by far!"

Still choking and gasping he put his free hand back beneath the surface and groped to tie the knot that secured the heavy rope around the colt's girth, just behind its forelegs. Reg picked up his end and laid it out straight, as if ready for a tug-of-war — which in a sense it was to be. Diana walked over and pointed to a spot.

"Will you stand here, Mrs. Ransome; and you here, Philip. Don't pull until we say so."

Reg went almost to the end of the rope, where there was a big tussock of moor grass, and picked it up, giving it a turn round his waist. Diana went in front of Mrs. Ransome, as near the mire as she could while still on fairly solid ground.

"All right, John," she said.

"Right," he answered, "just take the strain then."

"Gently," Diana said over her shoulder as they

took up the weight of the rope, "he's got to get its legs up now — tip it on to its side a bit. If he doesn't, and a leg is badly stuck down there, we could easily break it."

The boy shuddered. The colt's head was a blur now in the gathering darkness; John was hardly visible, but they heard the sucking of the mire as he went down again and yet again to raise the hidden legs, and the tortured gasping as he fought to breathe air rather than slime between submersions. At last he said, with difficulty, "All right. I'm coming."

They stood waiting, holding the rope firmly as he pulled himself back along its length. Looking like some troll from the darkness he scrambled on to the firm ground; still on his hands and knees he wiped his arms and face in the grass, like an animal. Then he stood up swiftly and moved over to Diana. Standing beside her he picked up the other light line that lay coiled on the grass and turned to peer at the others: he could just make out their shapes, tense and ready in the darkness.

"All right," he said sharply, "and let's hope he helps himself a bit. Give it everything you've got . . . Now!"

They threw themselves back against a dead weight. Their sinews cracking, their feet trampling on the soft going, they seemed to be pulling against a mountain. John was bent like a taut bow, pulling in one unremitting surge of power, the muscles standing up on his shoulders and down his spine; Reg hauled in a sort of frenzy, fighting and cursing; Diana, the boy, and

189

his mother threw their lesser strengths into the greater and strained to the point of nausea, but nothing moved, there was not even a tremor. John threw his head back without slackening his pull and yelled: "More! Come on, more!" and they gave it more, unbelievingly, having thought that there was no more, could be no more. The colt's head was stretched forward now by the line around its neck, yet its eyes were still sleepy and its breathing quiet: There was no sign of any fight in it and no sign of any giving anywhere of the black mire. Just as Philip felt tears start behind his eyes as he thought that the colt's neck must break, John threw down his line and gasped "Right!" They dropped the rope and slumped to the ground to regain their breath, all but John who remained standing, tense, half-crouched, facing the mire as though it were an enemy, defying it. Reg clambered to his feet, still wheezing heavily, and hobbled over to John.

"Pity us cud'n get thiccy car yur."

"Aye."

John's answer was fierce, but the old man knew that the anger was against the impersonal forces that opposed them. He gestured towards the motionless head, only dimly seen now:

"If awnly 'ee'd fight a liddle us'd 'ave un out."

John nodded grimly. Diana stood up and joined them.

"Poor devil must be exhausted — he's been in there for hours and it's *so* cold."

She shivered and looked back to where Philip was sitting, his arms clasped round his legs, his chin resting on his knees, not looking at the pony, looking anywhere but at the pony. She turned back to John and spoke urgently and quietly: "John, we must do something! We can't give up. Look at him!"

John and Reg both turned and looked; John was silent, but the old man shook his head and muttered again: "Tes a bliddy shame, I reckon, a bliddy shame."

John picked up the line with a sudden access of determination. "All right, let's try it again now that we've rested," he said clearly. They took up the rope and stood ready.

"Now!" he shouted.

The rope biting their hands, the treacherous ground slipping and balling beneath their feet, the breath painful in their lungs and harsh in their ears, the blood hammering in their temples, long seconds that stretched into minutes and hours as they fought the mire for its prize . . . and still the dim white head stretched forward calmly and remained still. This time Philip cracked. He choked suddenly and fell to the ground where he lay, his hands hiding his face, his body racked by sobs, or the effort not to cry. Diana and Mrs. Ransome both went to him and knelt by his side, waiting for the spasm to end. Reg went over to John again; they looked at each other and each knew what was in the other's mind: It wasn't going to happen. Philip was quiet now and was sitting as he had been before, facing away from the half-conscious colt. For a full minute there was no movement. They remained motionless in the silence of despair as the night wind trembled over them: John and the old man standing together looking at the boy as he sat hunched on the ground; Diana kneeling at his side, one hand resting on his shoulder; his mother standing before him, her hands hanging at her side, her head bowed in silent grief. Behind them, unseen and unseeing, the sad white head nodded once, then again, and the nostrils sank a little into the blackness; as the hidden ribs moved weakly a few bubbles frothed on the surface of the sline. Even the wind was silent.

Suddenly John smacked a fist into the palm of his hand: the others started, visibly.

"There's one more thing we can try — come on!"

He moved dynamically, rousing them from their apathy, getting them into their positions on the rope. He said to Reg, in an undertone: "I'm going in to wake him up, Reg."

The old man frowned once and said: "Yew tek care, midear."

John nodded and the old man wrapped the heavy rope round his waist and shuffled into his stance as they took the strain.

"Now!" John yelled, and as they heaved he plunged back into the mire and fought his way out to where the colt half-lay, quiescent, pulling himself along the quivering rope. He struggled to the colt's side and then erupted in an explosion of noise and energy:

"Hah-h-h!" he yelled, and again directly into the white ear "hah-h-h-h!" As he shouted he beat with his arms at the colt's head, its neck, at the surface of the mire, the sunken quarters, any-

192

where. The colt threw its head up sharply, its eyes suddenly wide.

"Hah-h-h!" savagely into the now-flickering ear, his teeth showing in a snarl as he beat the colt's neck, flat-handed but hard; all the while the rope strained and hauled and Reg's cursing sounded between John's yells.

There was a sudden tremor — then another: Reg felt himself topple then recover as the rope seemed to slide for a moment.

"Come on!" John shouted. He threw himself to one side and reached round under the mire for the colt's tail, found it, got both hands to it and heaved bodily, still yelling. All at once the colt seemed to come to life: the mud-spattered head reared back and it threw its forelegs forward, searching for firm ground.

"Keep it up!" John yelled. "He's coming!"

On land they sensed the transition from failure to success and threw themselves back, their feet scrambling for fresh footholds; Reg was too blown to curse, his eyes popping in the fury of his effort. Again the colt fought, struggling blindly forward: John sensed the legs thrashing perilously close to his own and he heaved forward again on the muscular tail; he heard the colt snorting and gasping as it used its last reserves of strength to fight the clinging mire, then it plunged forward. He felt the body move past him, heard the sucking noise as the bog surrendered its prize and floundered weakly after it to reach the firm going. It was all over; with a shuddering heave and scramble the colt reached safety and stood before them, breathing in great

193

gusts of air that whistled in its throat, its eyes half-closed again, its head hanging low. The sharp division between the white head and the black remainder gave it an alien disembodied look. John sat on the ground behind it, also recovering his breath, shaking his head and trying to grin; even his teeth were stained by the mire. The others had dropped the rope and moved in to form a group round the pony. Reg was trying to undo the knot behind its shoulder while Diana worked on the bowline round its neck. The boy was standing at its head stroking its forelock and ears; his mother stood just behind him looking down at him. The last faint radiance of the sun had been snuffed out in the west and the only sound apart from their breathing was the whispering of grass-stalks and stems of sedge as the bitter wind emphasied the depth of the night with its dark current of loneliness.

In their weariness they could have rested there for a while, but John knew that the battle was only half won: miles of difficult moor to cross with an exhausted pony that might not have sufficient reserves of strength to see it home on its own feet. Accordingly, as soon as he had recovered his breath, he got to his feet and faced the problem of the journey back to civilisation. The colt's bridle had been lost in the initial struggle into the mire; Reg now knotted a halter out of the light line and slipped it over the hanging head. Philip took it from the old man and tried to lift the colt's head a little, but without success.

Diana spoke quietly to John: "He must be

worn out after what he's been through; I'll lead the pony and he can go with you in the Rover."

John nodded. He went over to Philip.

"Philip, Diana will lead your pony and you can come with us in the car," expecting him to nod his compliance.

"N-no thanks. I'll t-t-take him m-myself," Philip replied out of the darkness. There was a moment of stunned silence as the words came clearly to all of them: the first words any of them had heard him say apart from his mother.

John acquiesced: "All right then; we'll see how you get along."

They set off on the first stage of the journey, back to the Land-Rover; John, Diana, and Mrs. Ransome walking ahead, Philip following with the colt and Reg bringing up the rear. It had been difficult to get the colt moving, but once started it walked with a clockwork regularity, broken by stumbling that grew less frequent as they progressed. At one point it tripped and fell quite heavily over a small rock showing just above the surface; it got up again quickly and stood snorting. John came back and ran his hand down its forelegs; it was difficult to tell through the fast-drying coat of mud, but he felt no damage. Philip, feeling the legs after him, found that they were trembling; laying his hand on the colt's neck, then its back, then its quarters, he realised that it was trembling all over. Disturbed, he jerked it into forward motion again, following the dim figures in front of him. By the time the lights of the Land-Rover came into view, pinpoints in the darkness, Philip was almost asleep on his feet; his legs worked mechanically, left, right, left, right with a hypnotic regularity. Once or twice the colt lurched forward striking his heel with one of its front hooves, but he hardly noticed the pain, only hurried forward a pace or two before falling again into his dreamlike progress.

When they arrived at the Land-Rover John immediately took out a rug and wrapped himself in it. Philip and the colt stood motionless, heads drooping, while decisions were made about the last stage of the journey. Again Diana suggested that Philip should travel in the vehicle, but he shook his head definitely, almost fiercely.

"I'll walk with him then," Diana said, but old Reg butted in testily.

"No, no, midear; I'm walkin' with young Philip yur an' you'm ridin' in thiccy car."

It was too cold to engage in long discussion: John gave the old man a torch so that he, in the Land-Rover, could keep in contact with them in case of accidents; he had serious doubts of Philip's ability to get back to the road before falling over with weariness but he knew that it would be useless to argue with the boy at this stage. Mrs. Ransome was anxious, seeing Philip sway slightly as he stood, half asleep, but she too knew that nothing would separate him from the colt now, unless it were the unconsciousness of sleep. The woman and the girl climbed into the vehicle while John had a last word with Reg.

"I'll have to go back by compass, Reg; it'd be a damn sight easier on foot but I can't leave the thing out here. You just keep that torch on so

196

that we can see you: I'll try not to get too far ahead. If you want help for any reason flash the torch on and off, all right? I'll get the girls to keep an eye on you."

"Yass, midear; doan'ee worry now."

"I shan't," John said, clambering awkwardly into the driving seat, swathed in his rug. The engine started into life, the gears grated, the headlights blazed suddenly cutting a swathe through the night, and then the car was bumping away from them like a squat chinese dragon. Philip stood bemused. The old man laid a hand on his shoulder and said: "Come along then, midear; 'tes a long way to go."

They all had a long way to go — all of them. Fairy stories can end so beautifully and so conclusively, but this one is about human beings.

As Philip and the old man moved off the moon was rising into a clear sky. The wind, which in the total darkness had been a tangible force, became transparent now as stars began to show through it one by one. It swept across the empty spaces like a great scythe cutting close to the ground and it was full of little cries of loneliness and sorrow. A dim silver radiance lay across the moor as if the earth itself were glowing faintly; it was enough to help the two of them to avoid rocks and clumps of heather, the pony following blindly, still stumbling occasionally.

In the Land-Rover the heater was humming loudly and warm air was already circulating, causing a delicious languor to steal up their limbs. Mrs. Ransome had tried to thank them.

"Doesn't matter," John said, hunched over the wheel. "Doesn't matter whose it is, if there's a pony stuck anywhere we'd get it out. And so would anyone else, come to that. It's a part of living where we do."

A little farther on Diana said: "I'm so glad that Philip's coming along so well."

The big woman nodded slowly, staring ahead down the beams of white light. "I thank God for it," she said quietly.

The vehicle rattled and bumped forward, the twin shafts of the headlights leaping and swinging as if invested with a life of their own.

The moorman turned in his bed, drifting restlessly between a feverish sleep and periods of clarity. He felt thin and insubstantial, as though he were floating a little way above his mattress; the bedclothes felt unbearably heavy and seemed to be pressing down on his chest, hampering his breathing. Sometimes a pain would come, shearing the fitful darkness with a spear of blinding light. The doctor was calling twice a day now and he was very ill.

Philip was walking in a dream: He felt as though he had lost his identity and only existed where he came into contact with the cold air and the ground, the rope to the colt's head, and the susurration of the wind. It was his concern for the pony that kept a focal point in his concentration; without that he would have drifted apart into fragments. His exhaustion had had a strange effect upon him: It had left him lucid and yet had removed his identity so that he seemed to be acting as an agent for himself . . . a sort of amanuensis, in full possession of the details of his life yet not personally involved. It was because of this that he had spoken to them all, there in the darkness. Now, with his legs swinging mechanically beneath him and the night wind playing in his hair, he knew what he had done and recognised its significance: Yet there was no sense of achievement. He merely accepted.

While John was outside checking his direction on the compass and looking around at the lie of the land, Mrs. Ransome asked Diana what they should do for the colt when they got it home.

"There's a shelter in the paddock, isn't there?" Diana asked. When Mrs. Ransome nodded she went on: "Then put him in there for the night. Shake down a lot of straw if you can. The vital thing is that he must be warm and the first thing to do is to rub his ears until they're dry and warm. If the ears are warm, the rest of the body is."

John came back and the uneven motion started again.

"Another very good thing is to put woollen bandages on his legs — leave them on all night. So long as he's warm . . . as soon as he's all right, turn him out again."

John glanced across at Diana and reminded her: "Don't forget the gruel."

"Oh yes, of course. Give him a gruel. Do you know how to make one?"

"I'm afraid not: I know nothing about horses."

"Well, I'm sure the Colonel will take charge and see the pony comfortable."

Mrs. Ransome turned towards Diana.

"But he's ill, didn't you know?"

"Oh . . . of course." Diana hesitated, then went on: "Then you've no one to help you?"

"Oh, we'll manage, don't you worry."

"Right, then," said Diana, "as soon as I've got John home I'll nip back and see the pony comfortable."

Mrs. Ransome protested: "No, Diana, you can't do that, it's ridiculous."

"It's not at all ridiculous, it won't take me more than a few minutes. If you'll put about half a bucket of water on to boil as soon as you get home, I'll bring some oatmeal. It's no good leaving a job half done."

Mrs. Ransome grimaced unhappily, but there was little she could do: She was incapable of seeing to the pony herself and she did not believe for a moment that Philip would even be awake by the time they finally arrived home.

The moorman woke from a brief but deep

sleep; his chest was on fire and there was a buzzing in his ears. I wonder what the time is, he thought. I wish to God I knew what was happening about that pony. I can't stand it if we've lost it, it'll be just too much.

Philip felt himself fall asleep for a split second: He felt the beautiful sense of peace begin to wash over him and then his mind tilted and jerked back to horizontal as he staggered sideways, arms out to save himself, letting go of the rope. Reg started forward but he recovered without falling and quickly retrieved the rope as the colt came to a halt, pulling it forward into unwilling motion again.

Old Reg walked behind the colt. As he went he was full of a sense of wonder at what he had experienced: hearing the silent boy utter those words. The others were happy about it, but to the old man it was something totally wonderful. He could think of nothing else. He watched the boy, walking dimly ahead of him, with eyes that were wide open and bright with a great gentleness. He longed to make some contact with the boy . . . he longed to say something to him and hear him answer. But he did not dare.

I'd forgotten the Colonel was ill, Diana was thinking. Of course, the boy's been looking after him, hasn't he?

"You know, it's strange," she said aloud, but to nobody in particular, "when you come to think about it: how the Colonel has been looking after

201

Philip all this time. And all of a sudden everything is turned round and now Philip's looking
after him. There's something so . . ." she
searched for a word, "so *right* about that, I don't
know why. Like repaying a kindness or something."

I had become so . . . still, so calm, the moorman thought: My life ran evenly and smoothly.
Yet this last year I seem to have blown up into
little pieces and fallen together again, anyhow.
I'd forgotten what it was like to suffer pain and
joy: all the good, searing, terrible emotions of my
youth. Bless the boy, he thought, there in the
darkness; he's stopped me growing old. He
smiled bleakly, then frowned again, shaking his
head, his eyes seeking the window that looked
out over the moors. What's happening out there?
What's going on . . . then the pain came again
and he let go of his thoughts so that he could
fight it.

Old Reg searched desperately for the right
thing to say. He was obsessed by now by the
desire to speak to the boy and fearful lest there
be no reply. His lips mumbled as he sorted over
various openings and he frowned at the pony's
quarters as its hooves went thud thud thud like a
dying heart. Suddenly the boy spoke.
"R-reg?"

The old man could not grasp it for a moment: His eyes stared and his mouth opened. Then joy, pure childlike joy flooded his being and shone from his face. He had almost halted in his confusion, now he hurried forward as the boy turned round, puzzled.

"Yass, yass, midear?" he scuttled forward to walk at the boy's side, as though he had been promoted.

"I j-just w-w-wanted to t-talk a little."

His voice sounded distant in his ears, and unfamiliar. He was content to let the old man talk, answering in monosyllables; like a tired fledgling, drowsily flapping its nearly hard-penned wings.

The moon was higher, details in the foreground were clearly visible now. The colt walked wearily, its eyes half closed, still trembling. The white head shone strangely in the silver moonlight, cut off from its body by the stark division where the mud had dried; to the boy's unfocused eyes it looked as though it were hanging there, the strangely glowing white head. The lashes were clearly visible, long and incredibly fine, so dense as to keep the moonlight out of the colt's eyes.

They were going slightly downhill now and the going was dryer.

"Not too long now," John said.

Mrs. Ransome looked at his profile: He was gazing intently at the ground ahead, his teeth still showing in the smile that he always wore when driving. She noticed the caked mud on the back of his hand and the wrist where it emerged from the rug. He's indestructible, she thought. Diana turned to look back for the wavering point of light behind them: it seemed to tremble slightly like a star low in the sky.

There's so much to think about . . . I seem to have learned so much about living this last year. Mrs. Ransome smiled slightly, the dim light from the dashboard showing the dimples that formed at each corner of her mouth. That sounds strange, doesn't it? I've learned a lot about living this year . . . like a song in the hit parade. But it's true. I feel as though I've become an entirely different person . . . as though I've become wider and deeper and . . . and slower somehow. Oh, and so much happier. And now we've made the break at last . . . Philip can talk to me now. Funny to think how often I've dreamed about this moment, and I never realised how . . . sort of ordinary it was going to be. Quite natural. No fuss. I suppose that's good though. . . .

The pain receded and the old man fought for breath, his eyes wide in the darkness. After a little while it seemed to ease somewhat. If they don't get that blessed pony out tonight it'll die, he thought. So might I. So what the hell? But I do care, he thought. Yes, I do care. I care most dreadfully. He smiled: Thank God for that, anyway: I still care.

Philip's eyes were closing and opening mechanically; very little was coming through from his legs; only delayed confused items of information. He did not know that Reg had quietly taken his arm and was half-supporting him. They were not talking now. Weariness was working on the old man too, but he was hardened to it and walked steadily, guiding the boy over the easier going. I wonder how the moorman is, Philip thought. I must go and see him later on — tell him everything's all right. A little later he thought: I hope there isn't too much farther to go.

The colt walked behind, connected by a piece of rope to the almost-sleeping boy. But by more than just this. The white colt had been a thread going through and through the boy's life ever since he had entered it that March day: a recurring motif in the design. The little falcon and the blue-eyed pony . . .

Yes, they had a long way to go, all of them. But the first lights of the village were rising like warm stars above the slope ahead of them. Soon they would be able to sleep off their weariness before going on again.